YOU GET WHAT YOU GIVE

A RETRO ROMANTIC COMEDY

CAROLINA CLASSICS
BOOK 1

KAREN GREY

Published by HOME COOKED BOOKS
A division of Jasper Productions, LLC
www.homecookedbooks.com

Cover artwork © 2022 by L.J. Anderson of Mayhem Cover Creations

ISBN: 978-1-7370383-7-5 (paperback)

ISBN: 978-1-7370383-6-8 (ebook)

Subjects: | BISAC: FICTION / Romance / Romantic Comedy. |

FICTION / Romance / Historical / American. |

First edition, June 2022

This is a work of fiction.

Names, characters and events are either a product of the author's imagination or are used fictitiously.

❀ Created with Vellum

PRAISE

★ ★ ★ ★ ★ "Loved the one-night stand plus enemies-to-lovers: 'oops the person I just slept with turns is now my biggest business rival--RIGHT NEXT DOOR.'" - *NYT bestselling author Cathryn Fox*

★ ★ ★ ★ ★ "Total trip back in time! Especially loved the instant chemistry & the winks to 90's pop culture." USA Today bestselling author Serena Bell

★ ★ ★ ★ ★ "This enemies-to-lovers, small-town retro romance is bursting with nineties pop-culture fun, deep-seated friendship, and lots of spice!" - *Bookbub review*

★ ★ ★ ★ ★ "I don't want to wait… to gush about this book! *You Get What You Give* by Karen Grey was a nostalgic romantic throwback to my teenage years that did crazy good things to my heart." - *Goodreads review*

★ ★ ★ ★ ★ "Smexy tension, banter and wonderful personalities." - *Bookbub review*

★ ★ ★ ★ ★ "Dust off your MMMbop cassette single and spritz on your Gap Grass fragrance spray we are going back to the 90s… When I say I loved this book I mean I LOVED it!!! It really did remind me of a 90s dramedy where one episode in an ensemble cast focuses on one couple." - *Goodreads review*

★ ★ ★ ★ ★ "As soon as I finished the prequel to the "Carolina Classics" series, I knew the series and characters were going to be all that and a bag of chips. *You Get What You Give* is a fun and nostalgic story set in the late 1990s that brought me back to my favorite era." - *Bookbub review*

★ ★ ★ ★ ★ "An absolute must-read… You'll be hooked and like me, chomping at the bit for the next book in the series!" - *Goodreads review*

CONTENT GUIDANCE

The content notes below are meant to give readers a generalized view of potentially triggering subjects within this novel.

- Use of expletives: frequent but not mean-spirited
- Sex/Nudity: several sex scenes on page
- Violence: none
- Alcohol use: multiple characters on page
- Recreational Drug use: main character (mention, in the past)
- Cigarette Smoking (off page)
- There is a guaranteed HFN but there is *also* a cliffhanger ending

If you'd like a more detailed list of content warnings (which may include spoilers) they are available at:

https://www.karengrey.com/contentguidance

"To love someone when there is no chance of that love ever thriving...that is romance."

—Joey, *Dawson's Creek*

"I wanted to write about falling in love and why it can't last, but at the same time how it lasts forever!"

—Dawson, *Dawson's Creek*

CHAPTER 1

Lawson's Reach "Pilot"

Parker is convinced that a video store customer was hitting on him. Lawson is skeptical, especially because the woman is older than they are.

VIOLET

When I find my friend Danielle's face behind the bar of the Rumrunner hotel, I head toward her like a heat-seeking missile. My mood must be clear because the moment she catches my eye she mouths, "The usual?"

By the time she finishes delivering drinks down the bar and mixing my White Russian, I've settled into a seat, but indignation still has me restless.

"Stop destroying my swizzle sticks," Dani says as she sets the glass of cold sweetness in front of me. "I can't believe you're still obsessed with these."

I lift my glass in a toast. "To *The Big Lebowski.* It's cast included some of the finest actors of our generation, and it taught me about the yummiest cocktail I've ever tasted.

"Where's your boy toy?" she asks while pulling a beer for

another customer. My job requires a certain amount of multi-tasking, but Dani's busier back there than ants at a picnic. However, she's bartended since the minute she turned twenty-one seven years ago, so she's able to listen while she works.

I stir my drink until the ice cubes spin. "That's an excellent question. He was supposed to meet me at Mediterraneo for dinner an hour ago, but he never showed."

"Bummer."

"Go ahead. You know you want to say it."

She just zips her lips.

"I know I should break up with him." I tick the reasons off on my fingers. "He's too young, he's not very smart, he's unreliable."

When she returns from delivering drinks, I finish the list. "But he's hella hot, and it would be mad awkward at the office if I broke up with him."

She just smiles and shrugs, but I know what she would say if she weren't so chill. "I know, I know. As soon as this is over, I'm swearing off baby surfer dudes."

"How old is he, anyway?"

I tap my chin. "Twenty-two, I think? When he first came in to sign up for work as an extra, I'm pretty sure he filled in his birth year as 1975."

"Six years between you is a dog's age," a bright and bubbly voice says behind me.

"Hey, girl. Whatcha drinkin'?" Dani asks Whitney—our other best friend—as she slips onto the barstool to my left. As per usual, guys up and down the bar stretch their necks to check her out. From her blond highlights to the big blue eyes made even bigger by artfully applied makeup, her look is designed to capture the male gaze, and it always does.

"A glass of chardonnay, please," Whit says primly before turning to me. "Thought I might find you here."

"You were looking for me?"

Biting a lined lower lip, she digs through the Fendi baguette she must have spent a ridiculous amount of money on. I mean, I love that new show *Sex and the City* too, but I can't afford to dress or accessorize like any of those women.

"When I dropped Skye at your place, Lance was there." Whitney slides a folded piece of paper across the bar, but when I try to take it, she won't let go. "You have to promise not to kill the messenger."

I snag the paper. After a quick perusal of what's written on it, I just shake my head. I should've known better. You never pair a leading man with a character actress.

"That bad?" Dani asks.

"What does it say?" Whitney whispers.

"You didn't look?" I ask her.

"I would never," Whitney protests. "But Lance did say he was afraid to tell you in person. He was just going to pin it to your door."

"Afraid? Of what?" I demand.

Whit flinches. "Of you yelling."

I blow out an impatient breath and pick up the piece of paper again.

"Did he break up with you?" Dani asks.

The White Russian is hitting the spot, but I push it away so I'm not tempted to gulp it down. "He not only broke up with me, he's moving to LA."

Which means I've lost my receptionist as well as my boyfriend—or whatever he was.

"Is this seat taken?"

I squeeze my eyes shut before answering the question posed from behind me. In fact, I find myself squeezing everything shut in response to the tone of that voice. Not that it's grating or bullish, the kind of voice that rubs me the wrong way. This man's luscious, mellow tone is catnip that has me wanting to rub against him.

Please be hideous, please be hideous, please be hideous, I chant

3

silently as I move my boho bag from the bar stool next to me. Armed with the Southern hospitality my grandma raised me to use, I scoot my seat away as much as I can in the crowded space. "It's all yours."

When I turn to look at him, the words *As am I* resound inside my skull. Where did they come from?

Let me count the ways.

First off, the dark-haired, five o'clock–shadowed guy with the sinful voice and a naughty look in his eye is a dead ringer for that guy from *Steel Magnolias* and *The Practice*, Dylan McDermott. I'd long ago shelved fantasies that the actor himself would shoot a movie in town and sweep me off my feet, but this guy's right here, and he smells like—

"Crowded for a Sunday night, huh?" That voice startles me back to reality. Man, I hope he didn't catch me sniffing him.

"Yeah," I agree, sounding like I've been huffing whip-its. "This place is always packed in the summer."

"That a White Russian?"

"Here's to The Dude," I say before draining the glass.

Get a grip, Violet.

Dani's empathetic frown shifts to a professional smile as she turns to the guy. "What can I get you, sir?"

Dylan-lookalike scans the taps and asks for a Sam Adams. While Dani pours his beer, I reach over the bar and squirt soda water into a glass, needing something that's neither sweet nor packing a punch to help me cool my jets.

Whitney pokes at the piece of paper, now sitting in a puddle of condensed water on the bar. "So, what did he say exactly?"

Humiliation heats my cheeks, so I take another gulp of water. "For starters, he said he didn't like how I bossed him around."

Whitney winces.

"I *am* his boss!" I protest. "Or I was."

"Maybe there's a lesson there?" Dani asks.

I snort. "Don't sleep with the help? Or with surfer dudes?"

"You are a bit intimidating, Vi," Whitney says. "I mean, *I'm* afraid of you sometimes, and I've known you since we wore training pants."

"Well, that's just stupid."

"Vi!" Dani admonishes.

"Proving my point," Whitney mutters.

I roll my eyes. "Sorry. I guess Lance won't have to be intimidated by me anymore. He's leaving tonight."

"Whoa." Dani's brows go up. "How long has he been planning this?"

"I don't know." I read over Lance's scrawl again. "It just says some guy told him he was driving to California, and Lance realized that if he didn't go for his dream, he'd always regret it. So he's going to Hollywood to be an actor."

"Jesus," Dylan says on a half laugh, half groan that has me wishing I could make that word come out of his mouth with lust instead of pity.

When I meet his sidelong gaze, he apologizes. "Sorry, don't mean to be eavesdropping, but"—he pauses for a moment to quickly look me up and down—"what an idiot."

"He was a jerk," Whitney adds, patting my arm.

"He's not a total asshole. Just kind of an airhead. A boy bimbo." I do my best to laugh it all off. "I guess it's my bad for trying to date above my pay grade."

My neighbor shakes his head and takes a sip of his beer. "The last thing LA needs is another actor wannabe."

A truism, but it sounds more personal for him.

"At least you won't have to see him again," Dani says, straightening and whipping a bar towel over her shoulder.

"Unless he actually gets work. Then I'll have to see him on the boob tube. With my luck, he'll book my favorite soap."

NATE

I'd been enjoying the show put on by the spitfire redhead next to me at the bar, but when she tells her friends about the guy that left her to go west to be an actor, I suddenly need more space than the crowded bar allows for.

Excusing myself as if I'm going to the restroom, I veer instead toward the lobby and the door that leads to the beach. When I checked into this oceanfront hotel two days ago, expecting to be able to watch the sunset over the waves, I had to remind myself that I'm now on the left coast. Lucky for me, instead of the Atlantic, my room faces the *other* body of water that flanks the island called Wrightsford Beach. In the time since my plane landed in the Wallington airport, I've heard several locals call it the "innercoastal" waterway, even though the sign reads "intracoastal."

One of many quirks I'm sure I'll discover during my stay in the city some are calling the Hollywood of the East.

After I find a lonely spot on the hotel deck, I lean on the faded wooden railing. A few deep breaths while staring at the great expanse of the ocean always calms me down, and after a few moments, I feel less agitated.

Unfortunately, that gives my dad's voice full rein inside my head.

You've got commitment issues, son. In the past four years, you've quit more jobs than I'll ever have.

After I finally graduated from college, which took an extra year because I transferred twice, I found a job that was as far away from Hollywood—and my father—as possible. It's true that I didn't last long at the first company, nor the ones that followed it. Each and every position I found was mind-numbingly tedious. Each time, I moved on. So sue me.

The joke my dad tells ad nauseum is that they based the movie *Reality Bites*—or *Singles* or *Kicking and Screaming*, all of which he cast, by the way—on my life. Which is totally unfair.

Or mostly unfair.

I don't get high every day. Anymore.

I am not a "master at the art of time suckage." I can get a lot done when I want to.

I may know all the words to "Conjunction Junction," but I can also make a kick-ass spreadsheet.

I just haven't found the thing that makes me want to settle.

Or maybe growing up in and around Hollywood just ruined me for the real world. Making widgets is boring. He was right about that.

Long story short, when my family decided to add Wallington to our ever-growing list of satellite offices, taking on the project of getting it open seemed like a way to show him that I'm no longer the screw-up stoner-surfer I was in high school.

His response when I asked for the job?

Sure, what the hell. Even you couldn't screw this up, Nate.

That's about the highest praise anyone gets from my father. Unless you're my older sister Monica. She's always been the golden child. Straight As from kindergarten to college had her coasting into law school at UCLA. Now she's my dad's right hand. He even changed the name of the business from Fowler Casting to Fowler Stern Casting, adding her married name. She negotiates all the deals with agents and producers, getting the company producer credits and royalties in return for my dad's connections with the hottest actors, while her actor husband mostly stays home with the kids.

I'm just not like them. Or anyone else in my family. Even my cousin Jay, heir to his father's casting dynasty in New York and Boston, delights in rubbing elbows with Broadway stars. Meanwhile, I'd rather spend my days doing anything on the water.

In fact, at the moment I'm regretting leaving my boards in a storage unit back in Santa Monica. But something in me needs to prove to my dad—and maybe to myself—that I'm at the very least responsible enough to run a casting office in this backwater town.

How hard can it be? The Beverly Hills office will handle all of the top-of-show and headliner casting. All I have to do is find local actors to fill small roles. In LA, you have to beat them off with a stick. Sure, the pool won't be as large here, and maybe the serious ones do go west, like the guy who broke up with the redhead, but I read up on this town before flying east. It's served as a location for a growing number of B-movies and even a couple of blockbusters. That kind of success must draw actors as well as stage crew members.

I mean, who wouldn't want to work in a place like this instead of smog- and traffic-clogged Los Angeles?

And if all the women are as charming as that girl at the bar, I might even want to stay awhile.

Just don't run away again, okay, Natie?

That was my sister. She's usually on my side, despite the fact that my dad treats me like I don't belong in the family business, or even in the family at all. This may be my last chance to prove him wrong. One way or the other.

VIOLET

After the hot guy excuses himself to visit the facilities, I try to get Dani's attention. By the time she finishes helping customers at the other end of the bar, I'm bouncing on my barstool with impatience.

"You need another drink already?" she asks, as she clears my empty glass.

"No, I'm good, but listen." I draw a circle in the air

between my friends and me and lower my voice. "Can we have a little girl-to-girl check-in about that guy?"

Dani raises a brow. "You mean as opposed to a bartender-to-customer check-in?"

"Yeah. Except we've never really had that relationship. I mean, I was your boss here."

"For one summer," Whitney points out.

"It was almost half a year," I say.

"If you want to do this 'check-in,'" Dani says as she opens the dishwasher, releasing a cloud of steam that momentarily separates us, "you'd best get to it because I do have other actual paying customers. Besides, he could be back any minute."

After a quick look over my shoulder to make sure he's not indeed walking our way, I whisper, "I just wanted to find out if either of y'all were into him before I make a move."

"Which guy are we talking about?" Whitney asks. She's been flirting with two guys standing behind her for the past ten minutes, but if she were to turn her attention on Dylan's doppelgänger, I'd lose him in two seconds flat.

I point to the empty seat on my right. "That guy."

Dani cocks her head to the side as she dries a glass. "He is pretty cute."

"Pretty cute?" Whit says, fanning herself with a coaster. "He's bangin' hot."

"Okay," I say, doing my best to squelch my disappointment. "Forget it."

"I'm not saying I'm into him," Dani says. "He's not really my catnip."

"Do you even have a catnip? Like, have you taken that diaphragm out for a test drive?"

Dani looks around, her eyes wild. "Jesus, Violet. Just announce my private business to the entire bar."

"I just think that using a diaphragm on top of the pill, plus asking the guy to use a condom is a bit much. I was

KAREN GREY

there when the Planned Parenthood lady explained that to you."

Whitney scrunches up her button nose, which makes her look even cuter. "Lord have mercy, Dani. Is that what you do?"

"I'm not talking about this while I'm at work," she hisses. "But I'll tell you one thing that's for sure: No way am I having a one-night stand with a traveling salesman."

"Is that what he is?" Whitney asks.

Dani shrugs. "He sure ain't from around here. He put his drink on his room tab, so I know he's staying at the hotel. And that suit he's wearing? Looks expensive."

"Maybe he's here for a job interview," I say.

"Where would a guy with a suit like that work around here?" Whitney shakes her head definitively. "Trust me, he did not get that at Belk's."

She's right. Wallington's rich people are old-money types who'd only wear seersucker this time of year. Between UNCW and the growing retiree population, professors and doctors make up our white-collar contingent, but I didn't get either of those vibes from him.

"Maybe he's some sort of engineer here to work at GE," I suggest.

Dani throws a bar towel over her shoulder. "My bet is pharmaceutical rep. But it doesn't matter. With my family's track record, if I even looked at him sideways, I'd get pregnant." The whirlwind of pouring, shaking, wiping, and serving stops for a moment, and she lays both hands on the bar. "You know what I'd love? If there was some sort of crystal-clear sign so you'd know exactly when you were ovulating."

"Like you turned blue?"

"Maybe not that extreme. Maybe just a little dot that lit up."

"I can see that introducing all kinds of problems."

"Guys could have one too."

"With their sperm count?"

"Yeah. Then everyone would know what they were getting into."

"What about romance?" Whitney asks.

Dani wags a finger back and forth. "There ain't no romance that can survive spitting out a kid every ten months like every other woman in my family does. Everyone except Aunt Doris, of course. May she rest in peace."

Dani moved out of her crowded family home years ago to live with her "poor" maiden aunt Doris, who was, according to my dear friend, the happiest Goodwin in the county. When she passed away a couple years ago, she left her home to her favorite niece.

"Well, I've got plenty of condoms, and I'm on the pill. I'm thinking…" I check over my shoulder again and catch sight of a certain tall, dark, and handsome man threading through the crowd. Leaning across the bar, I whisper, "I'm thinking a one-night stand with a not-here-for-long guy is exactly what I need to bounce back."

Dani frowns. "What about just going home and getting a good night's sleep? You do have a business to run."

"That *would* be the wise thing to do…" I say, dragging out the word "wise."

Whitney giggles. "But that's not what you're gonna do?"

"I don't think so," I sing-song. "Anyway, things are going great at work. The producers were totally jazzed about the actors I got them for the first two episodes of *Lawson's Reach*. I've got everything at the office under control. I will have to find a new receptionist to replace Lance, but that's not happening tonight. I could just use a little ego boost." I place a restraining hand on Whit's arm. "You know that if you even blink at him sideways, it'll be over for me."

"Oh, don't be silly, Vi. But don't worry"—she glances at

something behind me before leaning close to whisper—"he's all yours."

Just then, Dylan Twin—I really should get the guy's name if I'm going to seduce him—eases into the chair next to me and takes a sip of his beer. Ratcheting up my performance a hair, I say, "Pshaw, I totally dodged a bullet with Lance. If I stuck with a flake like him, I'd be cleaning up his messes the rest of my life."

Dani points her soda gun at me before filling a glass. "Which is what happens when you get married, no matter who it is."

Whitney sighs. "Such a cynic."

"Just know a lot of examples," Dani mutters as she heads to the other end of the bar to deal with a waving cocktail waitress.

My prey is staring off into space, so I offer up my hand. "Hey, I'm Violet. Welcome to Wallington."

He smiles, and an honest-to-god dimple appears. "Thanks. I'm Nate. Nathaniel. Either one."

We shake hands, and I'm rewarded with a little zing that tells me I'm not totally off base. There *is* something between us. "You don't have a preference?"

"Nope." He releases my hand, but swivels to face me. "But I thought this was Wrightsford Beach."

"It is." I wave a hand in a north-to-south direction over my head. "This island and a chunk of land on the other side of the intracoastal make up Wrightsford Beach. But it butts up against Wallington, and they're both part of New Hanover County, so most people call the whole area Wallington."

Before I can ask what he's doing in town, Dani swoops back in.

"I have a theory about you and men, you know," she says, ignoring my wide-eyed message: *I'm busy here.* "You control everything else in your life to the nth degree. But men? They're like cute little puppies, and you're the fire hydrant."

I glance at Nate with a nervous laugh. "I don't think I like where this is going."

"They drain you dry, and then they pee on you."

Whitney gasps. "Dani, ew!"

"Metaphorically," Dani concedes.

I turn to Nate with what I hope is an unruffled smile. "Please excuse my friend and her graphic analogy. Which is totally off, by the way."

"At the very least you could stop dating younger men," Dani mutters.

"All the older local guys are taken. Or boring." I place a flirty hand on Nate's forearm, doing my best to get back on track. "Sorry, no offense."

"Well, I'm not local and… how old do you think I am?"

Whitney and I look him up and down before answering in unison, "Thirty-five."

Nate almost chokes on the last of his beer. "I'm *twenty-five*."

"Really? No way."

"You do seem older," Dani nods. "At least not younger than us. We're twenty-eight."

"Thanks, I guess?"

Whitney leans forward to catch his eye across the bar. "I mean, you are wearing a business suit."

He smooths a tie that doesn't need smoothing. "I'm in town on business."

Dani shakes her head. "Honey, this is a beach town. Unless you're in court pleading for your life or somebody else's, or that life's over and you're in a funeral home saying goodbye, nobody wears a suit."

I tap my knee to his. "My dentist wears shorts under his lab coat."

He straightens but doesn't move his knee. "Where I'm from, there's a class line between suits and shorts."

"Not here," I say, turning to face him fully, letting my knee skim along the length of his thigh. "You button up for church on Sunday, but that's it. And even then, you just wear a nice pair of khakis and a button-down. Short sleeves in summer, long in winter."

"I'll keep that in mind," he says with what I am pretty darn sure is a flirty smile.

CHAPTER 2

Lawson's Reach "Pilot"

When Lawson invites Charli to sleep over, she's not sure it's a good idea.

NATE

I may be a fuck-up in my family's eyes, but I've never had a hard time finding girls to hang out with. The problem has always been keeping them. My sister says I'm afraid to find out what'll happen if I stick around long enough to get beyond casual hookups, but she's hardly a paragon of relationship success. It's obvious to everyone but her that she and her husband have problems.

I should probably be focusing on plans for my first full day at the office tomorrow, but I literally can't take my eyes off this Violet girl. From her hoot of a laugh to the freckles across the bridge of her nose to her sharp tongue, she's adorable. That actor who traded her for Hollywood is going to be kicking himself for letting her go, especially when he inevitably crashes and burns.

His loss and my gain. I haven't had this much fun just

talking to a woman since… well, ever. I can only imagine how the sparks would fly if we moved things between the sheets.

When she decides to pack it in for the night, I tell myself I want to be sure she's okay to drive. As far as I can tell, she only had the one drink, but I'm just not ready to say goodbye.

I sign off on my tab and step away from the bar. "Let me walk you to your car."

"Oh, that's not necessary."

"Of course it is," I say, following her to the lobby. "It's late, and it's dark."

She pauses in front of the guest services desk. "Wallington is a city only in name."

"That may be true, but this place is full of out-of-towners who've been drinking too much. I may be from elsewhere, but I've only had one beer." I hold out a crooked elbow. "Humor me?"

She takes my arm. "Well, that is very gentlemanly of you."

After we pass through the automatic doors into the still-humid air of the parking lot, I let the truth escape. "You wouldn't say that if you knew what I was thinking."

"Oh, and what is that?"

Her tone is as flirtatious as the looks she's been giving me all night, but I need to be sure, so I release her elbow. "Let's just leave it there, so you can go home thinking I'm a good guy."

She leans against a car, one brow raised.

"The guy that broke up with you." I shrug. "He's blind *and* an idiot."

She tips her head to the side. "You up for propping up my ego a bit more?"

"What did you have in mind?"

"I think it's the same thing you have in mind." Her voice has dropped in pitch, making it even sexier. "I mean, I could be up for a nightcap. In your room."

I nod slowly. "The only thing that's going to happen if you come to my room doesn't involve drinking."

"Maybe that's what I'm suggesting, in a roundabout way." She picks up the end of my tie and begins to reel me in, her eyes never leaving mine. "Give a girl a break here. She just got ditched."

I lean back until the fabric is a taut line between us. "I could be a good guy and walk away right now."

"Or you could be a bad boy…?"

"That'd make you very happy."

"Hmm. Maybe I need a taste bef—" Instead of finishing her sentence, she grabs one of my hands and captures a finger with her teeth. When her tongue curls around it, I think I might explode.

After dragging my finger past her lips, I grasp both sides of her face and bring my mouth within a hair's breadth of hers. Inhaling her sweet scent, I brush my lips across hers. Once, twice… but before I get to the third, what needs to happen is crystal clear.

She's soft, but strong.

I'm hard and deliciously powerless here.

Panting, I pull away, "I'm up for whatever you are."

"Let's go get naked, then," she whispers.

VIOLET

I mean, I do usually have at least one date with a guy before ripping my clothes off, but—fuck it. If someone's going to call me bossy, I may as well embrace the persona. Besides, I've got another stressful sixty-hour work week ahead of me, so I could use a little Sunday night pick-me-up.

So far, mission accomplished.

Insistent fingers spear through my hair. Equally eager lips, teeth, and tongue caress and nip and lick their merry way over my skin. Since the moment the heavy hotel door thunked shut behind me, this gorgeous man has had me pressed up against it to worship every inch of my mouth, neck, and shoulders.

He's winding me up, and I want more, faster. I push him away from the door. "Move it along, cowboy."

When he stumbles back, hands in the air, I can't help but laugh. "This isn't a stick-up."

"You've stolen something from me, that's for sure."

He's still walking backwards into the room, so I grab ahold of his lapels. "Just so you know, I don't usually make a habit of one-night-stands."

He stops and looks down at my hands briefly before meeting my gaze with a wicked smile. "Yeah?"

"I mean, I do like to get to know a guy first." Hesitation may ride my words, but my hands are busy belying them, pulling him so close there's only breath between us. "But I could be convinced to make an exception."

"Well," in between dotting featherlight kisses across my jaw, he whispers, "We can get to know each other." *Kiss.* "Tell me something." *Kiss.* "I'd know about you." *Kiss.* "If we talked all night."

Kiss.

Knees weak, sex wet, I can only come up with, "Uhhh…um."

He moves to my neck. "How about I start?" *Kiss.*

"Good idea," I manage.

"My…" *Kiss.* "Zodiac sign is Aquarius." *Kiss.* "I don't like chocolate." *Kiss.* "And my favorite color is green. The green of your eyes, in fact."

He leans back to meet my eyes, which are likely mostly black at the moment I am so turned on.

Swallowing, I do my best to find my words, but when he lifts my hand and begins to kiss his way up my arm, I lose the game of hide and seek. "I… like… um… kissing."

He pauses at my inner elbow, and the corners of his mouth lift. "Good to know."

"Good to be known." My voice is as wobbly as my knees. "Oh, and I'll eat *all* the chocolate."

Sadly, he releases my hand. Happily, he uses the opportunity to shrug out of his suit coat and toss it over a chair. Then he reaches for the side zipper of my dress. "May I?"

"Oh yes, you may."

As he slides the zipper down, I fumble with the buttons of his dress shirt.

Swallowing, his Adam's apple bobbing, he pulls at his tie. Before he can take it off, I stop him. "Leave that for last. It's growing on me. The shirt needs to go, though," I say, my voice huskier than usual.

Deft fingers make quick work of the rest of his buttons, and he tosses his shirt aside too, but of course he's got a Hanes underneath it.

The wickedness is back in his grin when he nods at me. "Your turn."

I reach down to unhook the strap of my heels, but he stops me with an *ah-ah* that I'd use to warn my dog off the couch. "Those have grown on *me*. Take something else off."

Pressing my lips into a pout, I fling a hand at him. "No fair. You've got like—" I pause to scan the broad shoulders, lean torso, and long legs before me. "Five more things to take off. I'm way ahead of you."

He scans me up and down, the perusal so slow and thorough that I'm reminded of his hands on me when we were out in the parking lot, of the way they seemed to approve of my generous figure. I can't take it anymore, so I shake my head. "Done with this."

His face falls. "Done?"

"Let's see if I can be clearer." Crossing to him, I unbuckle his belt and shove his dress pants down before whipping my dress over my head. As I toss it aside, his gaze locks on my cleavage.

Thank you, Victoria's Secret.

I point at his feet. "Shoes off, shorts off. Everything off but the tie."

I lean in to nip his full lower lip before growling, "Then meet me on the bed."

NATE

I have never met a woman like Violet. It's not just that she's a Carolina girl and I'm used to the ones in California. She's in a whole other category.

She strips down to nothing but scraps of lace that barely contain the contours of her hips and breasts, whips the covers off the king-sized bed like a warrior princess, and I'm ready to be conquered.

Not that there was a question that I'd be into her. I've had a rocket in my pocket since she brushed her knee against mine in the bar. In the parking lot, when she stepped close enough that I could detect her scent—freesia, maybe, and whatever pheromones smell like—I was a goner.

Now that I'm free of shirts and shoes and slacks, but still wearing the tie she mocked in the bar, she uses it to pull me on top of her.

I may be a bit of a loner—"disaffected loser" would be my dad's wording—but it's easy to connect with a gorgeous woman once we're skin to skin, so I take a trip down south on this luscious body. All worries about the week ahead disappear as her skin shudders underneath my lips.

In fact, her sweet-but-not-too-sweet scent erases all thought.

VIOLET

Most guys go straight for my boobs. I mean, I guess they're pretty special. And I do pay beaucoup dollars to have them lifted and shoved together in what is apparently an appealing fashion to the rougher sex.

But this guy? After a brief pass, his mouth keeps going.

Which I ain't gonna complain about.

His teeth find the lacy bit of lingerie that barely covers the red hair underneath that I keep trimmed but not waxed. Any guy that wants bare down there is basically a pedophile, in my opinion. When he teases those curls away from the place my friends and I call the Butter Bean, I shudder with raw need. Then another finger joins his teeth to inch the thong down my hips. Impatient as always, I can't not help, so I lift my hips.

The corners of his lips lift in an expression that matches mine. Like we've gotten away with eating the last slice of pie. Making quick work of my thong and tossing it over his shoulder, he grabs my hips and pulls me to the edge of the bed with surprising strength. A giggle slips out of me as he shoves my knees wide and kneels on the floor.

Hands stroke up and down my thighs, thumbs getting closer and closer to the finish line. Before I can even think of a word or two of direction—something most guys need—fingers curl deep inside, his tongue finds the Butter Bean…

And every single one of my cells clenches. A moan of pure lust grits out of me. His growl in response vibrates on my pleasure zone like no battery-operated device ever could. When he taps the old G-spot as he sucks on the Bean, I go nuclear, shock waves blasting from top to bottom and back again.

"Condom," I manage, my voice thready and probably way too needy.

After a last little massage that spreads my girly wetness around like he's planning to make good use of it, he sprints to the bathroom. Before I can have a little debate over why some guys keep 'em in their wallet and others in their dopp kits, he's back, and I use the tie—the thing really is handy—to pull him close. Then, eyes on the prize, I grab the condom, rip open the foil, and have it covering his impressively long, hard, and ready-to-go erection before you can say Jack Robinson.

He shoves me onto my back. I scoot across the bed. He follows, a tiger on my tail. I let him catch me and then he's inside. Not slow, not gradual, not gentle. He just homes in on his target and blasts me to kingdom come.

NATE

Panting, soaked in sweat, it takes a good long time for my brain to reboot after I collapse half-on, half-off of Violet. I probably look like a wacked-out zombie, but for once, I don't give a shit.

In LA, every guy is perfect. Coiffed, gym-toned, moisturized. Their colored contact lenses match their shirts. To make matters worse, once a pretty actress figures out that I can't get her a job even though my family runs a casting company, I'm dead in the water.

But this girl. My mind's so fried from whatever that was that I. Cannot. Compute. She called this a one-night stand, but all I can think right now is if I get the chance to do *that* again, I'll take it.

Eventually, my heart rate slows, and my immediate need

involves getting rid of the condom, so I whisper a "Be right back" and head to the bathroom to toss it.

When I return, a sliver of moonlight cuts through the drapes, the perfect lighting for her creamy skin. I slip back onto the bed, unsure if she's fallen asleep. Her hand finds mine and tells it she wants more attention. My palm obeys, stroking gently over soft skin. She actually purrs as I stroke over a shoulder, a hip, a calf. Just as my little guy is thinking he might be up for another round, an "Oh, crap" startles me away from her.

She slaps a hand to her face, and then the other joins it to scrub. "Ugh."

"Is everything okay?"

She blows out an impatient breath. "Yes. But no. I'm just a shit puppy mom." She leans over to give me a totally unsatisfying peck on the cheek, and before I know it, the bathroom door closes behind her. I'm still sitting there, stunned, when she emerges, seeking and finding her clothes, covering that Venus-like body, a rueful smile creasing her face.

"This was great. I mean it. And maybe we can do it again sometime if you come back in town, but right now, I gotta go."

CHAPTER 3

Lawson's Reach "Pilot"

Lawson is happily surprised to learn that he has an attractive new neighbor.

VIOLET

I'm a little late getting going the morning after what I think—no, I *know*—qualifies as the best one-night stand I've ever had. Not that I've had that many. It's not always the smartest thing to do, safety-wise. Plus, I know practically everyone in town. Don't want my favorite restaurant ruined because I slept with the bartender.

But this was a little beyond no-regrets territory. I actually felt a connection to this guy. One of those we-must-have-known-each-other-in-another-life kind of things. Not that I believe in that nonsense, but I don't know how else to explain the ease between us. And once we got our clothes off, the fireworks.

Chemistry, I guess?

"Your dog's eating my flowers, Violet!"

Our neighbor startles me from my reverie. "I'm so sorry,

ma'am. Skye, off!" The puppy cringes, poor thing. It's not her fault I've just been standing on the sidewalk mooning off into space.

"Everything all right, dear?"

"Everything's great. How are your tomatoes this year?"

After a lengthy conversation about hornworms, I'm rewarded with a shopping bag full of still-warm-from-the-sun and smelling-like-summer Big Boys, but time is a-wastin'. "Shoot, I've got to get going."

"Tell your grandparents I said hello."

"I will. Let's go, Skye." Hustling my dog into the car, I do my best to push nagging worries about my grandparents to the back of my mind. They're getting up there, and running their inn has become more challenging for them. I live in the carriage house apartment in the back, so I'm always there if they need me. Which, unfortunately, has happened more often of late. I keep finding cleaning supplies forgotten in the oddest places, for one, and the other day my grandpa must've mistaken the baking soda for baking powder, because the muffins at breakfast were inedible.

But right now, I'm determined to enjoy what life has served up for me. It's a glorious summer morning, I'm sexually satisfied, and all my best friends are finally in one place again. Lance is in my rear view, and "I've got the best puppy in the world, don't I?"

Skye agrees with the cutest little "arf" ever.

I may be late, but I still need my morning caffeine, so I stop by Deluxe and pick up a large cup to go.

After I make the turn from 23rd Street and park in my reserved spot at the front of the studio lot, I stop by the security booth.

"How you doin', Miss Violet?" the older gentleman who works the day shift asks.

In the past, when I contracted with the Fowlers in New York to do background casting on a project-to-project basis, I only rented an office short-term. Now that I've got a show to cast for a full nine months, I'm in for a full year. "I'm awesome, Sam. Did you have a nice weekend?"

It makes his job easier if he knows I have actors coming for auditions, so after I hear all about his visit with his grand-kids, I fill him in on my schedule for the day.

Then I walk Skye over to a strip of grass so she can do her business one more time before we head inside to face the phones. "If there's no chewing on the office furniture today, I'll take you to the beach after work," I tell her. "Maybe we'll run into that cute guy from last night."

As we round the corner of the long aluminum-sided building that houses various production offices, my imagina-tion must be playing tricks with me, because a man that looks a hell of a lot like that cute guy from last night strolls toward us. When we get close enough that Skye lets out what is prob-ably meant to be a warning bark but is really a high-pitched yip, the man stops.

Well, I'll be dipped and rolled in cracker crumbs. It is him.

"Hey, Nate. Uh, what are you doing here?" I ask, doing my best to keep my tone even. He didn't give off a stalker vibe the night before, but as Dani pointed out, my judgement with men isn't the greatest.

His smile is as confused as mine is forced. "Uh, this is where I work."

Skye barks at him again.

"Who's this?" He reaches down to pet her, but she growls at him. Straightening, he meets my gaze. "Not friendly?"

"Usually, she's very friendly. Enough, Skye." I use the stern tone our trainer Lucy taught me. "Down."

With a grunt that I swear sounds like a teenager's "Fine," she settles onto the sidewalk.

"I see you went with the suit again," I can't help but point out.

He frowns, making me wonder if he thinks *I'm* stalking

him. "Yeah, suits are the only thing I packed appropriate for work."

"Well, nice to see you again." What exactly is the protocol for running into a one-night stand at one's place of business? Pretend that he hasn't seen me naked? That I don't want to kiss that frown off his face?

When we both take a step toward the same glass doors, I almost choke on my own spit, I'm so flabbergasted. "You're working in this actual building?"

He pulls a slim calendar from his breast pocket, consults it, and checks the list of office numbers listed on the sign over the doors. "I'm going to One-C."

"One-C is empty." In fact, I was hoping to be able to expand into it someday.

He pulls a set of keys from his pocket and holds them up. "Not anymore."

"Huh," I say, suspicion creeping back into my gut. "What a coincidence. That's right next door to my office."

After a somewhat awkward pause, he steps in front of me to open the door, gesturing for me to precede him.

"Let's go, girl," I say to Skye as we pass through. I catch a whiff of his aftershave, something spicy that brings up very detailed memories from last night's tryst. Even though the AC is pumping cool air overhead, I can feel the heat of him as he follows me down the hall.

"Well, welcome to the building," I say as I unlock my door. The phone's ringing on the other side, so I give him a little wave. "I've got to get in there, but we should, uh… have lunch sometime."

He stares at the sign over my door for a moment before saying, "I'm not sure how long I'll be here."

Before I can rearrange my face to hide my disappointment, he adds, "But yes, I'd like that."

NATE

The carved wooden sign over Violet's office door features a rod, reel and fishing line arcing over wooden letters proclaiming "Casting Carolina." The words set off warning bells. I mean, it seems pretty odd that a fishing supply store would be located on the periphery of a film and TV production facility. But what do I know? There *is* a lot of water around here. The county jail's just down the street, with a bail bond and pawn shop nearby. I suppose it's possible hers is just another in a ragtag collection of businesses that ended up on this stretch of road outside of town.

It does rattle me that the woman I was so happily naked with just hours ago is right next door. I'd literally been wondering if and how I'd find her again when I saw her striding up the sidewalk, but something tells me that the coincidence is too good to be true.

At the moment, however, work beckons. Violet's phones aren't the only ones ringing off the hook. When I step inside —still a bit discombobulated—the answering machine is taking a message, so I hustle to unpack my briefcase and get started.

The previous tenant left behind a few things, but I need more than desks, chairs, and bookcases to get a casting office outfitted. After flying in on Friday, I spent Saturday driving around picking up basics. The good thing about Wallington, I learned, is that its small size means that anything and everything is only a fifteen-minute drive away. The bad thing is that anything and everything is missing a few essentials.

I'll have to wait on delivery of the computers I ordered, but the file cabinets I picked up are ready to be filled with actor headshots and résumés, and the fax machine is spitting out what looks like a script.

Tossing keys and briefcase on the desk and ripping the plastic off a stack of legal pads, I perk up when the current caller announces herself as the California production coordinator for *Lawson's Reach*. Picking up before she finishes with her message, I say, "Carolina Casting. Nathaniel speaking."

"This is Carolina Casting?" she asks, emphasizing each word.

Didn't I just say that? Maybe I'm more out of it than I thought. "It is."

"Sorry, it's early here, and I… just want to be sure I've got the right place."

"I'll admit I didn't expect the California office to be calling at 6:00 a.m."

"You and me both, dude."

"What's up?"

"Hate to be the bearer of bad news, but we've got a rewrite. We could fly an actor in from here to fill the role, but it's only a couple of lines—"

Overly eager to prove my worth, I jump in. "Whatever you need, we'll find it." Of course, the "we" is just me at the moment. But she doesn't need to know that.

After she gives me the details and I hang up, I realize that since I don't have a computer and printer, I can't type up a submission to fax to Breakdown Services. And even if I could, the information wouldn't get to agents fast enough. I need to get actors in here and auditions recorded tomorrow so I can overnight them to LA for approval.

I suppose now is as good a time as any to introduce myself to the local talent agents. One of our assistants back at Fowler Stern pulled together a list for me, and there are only a handful in the entire state, so at least it won't take long.

I dial the number that has the Wallington area code first. After I introduce myself and tell her what I'm looking for, she asks, "What did you say the name of the show was?"

"It's called *Lawson's Reach*. It's on the BW? The new Brothers Werner subsidiary? The pilot was shot here and—"

"Okay, right. I know. Can I put you on hold for a sec?"

As inane hold music blares, I regret not stopping somewhere on the way to work to get a cup of coffee. The thin brew I made back at the hotel room is not going to get me through the day. As I write "Buy coffee maker" on my growing to-do list, I remember that Violet was carrying a to-go cup. Asking her for a recommendation might be a good excuse for a visit next door. We could take a coffee break together.

"Hey," the agent says, breaking into my thoughts, "I'm sorry, did you say Casting Carolina?"

"No, Carolina Casting."

"Well, call me confused. Four of my young women are reading for that show this afternoon. At *Casting Carolina*," she repeats, emphasizing the word order. "Did y'all change the name since last week?"

The roar inside my head—louder than the surf at its roughest—is so deafening that it takes a moment for her words to break through.

"Hello? Are you still there?"

"I'm here," I answer, suddenly exhausted.

"What should I tell these actresses?"

"Uh. Yeah—I mean, not—no. I—I'll get back to you."

The dial tone echoes in my ears as I resign myself to the very real possibility that my family—aka my father—has stirred up a hornet's nest here without warning me about it. It'd serve him right if I just packed it all up and left.

VIOLET

The first call I make once I get settled is one I should've made last night. Since Dani and Whitney are both working today, I'll have to call in a favor with one of the guys.

"Good morning, Ford," I say cheerily when my buddy answers. "What are you up to today?"

"Not much," he says on a yawn. "I'm still pretty beat from going out on the boat last night with Sully."

No need to mention that I was out pretty late myself. Ford is pretty protective of Dani, Whitney, and me. "Any chance you'd want to come and answer phones for me today?"

"What happened to the guy that does that for you?"

"It's a long story, and I'm busier than expected. Please? I'll make you dinner."

"No thanks. I value my digestive system too much for that."

"Ford, please—"

"I'll answer your phones. But you're taking me *out* to dinner."

"I can do that."

"See you in a few."

Dani, Whitney, Sully, Ford, and I have been close since kindergarten. They're still my best friends, but while Dani and Whitney and I stayed in Wallington after college, Sully and Ford took off for Los Angeles. They've visited over the years, of course, since their families are still in town. But this year, they returned to work on a movie here in town from March to May. Having them around has made life so much sweeter, and since that movie wrapped, I've been on tenterhooks waiting for them to decide whether to make the move home permanent.

Sully dove right back into life here, pulling his old boat out of storage and hitting the beach daily to surf. But Ford seems less settled.

He still has an apartment in Los Angeles, so he's been couch surfing while he decides whether to go back to California or try to get on another show in Wallington. I'm voting for the latter, of course. In fact, maybe being on the lot today will convince him that the film and TV business has grown since he moved away seven years ago.

Buoyed by that thought, I begin working my way through answering machine messages in between fielding incoming calls. By the time Ford walks in, the phones have calmed a bit, but I've got a to-do list as long as my arm. I quickly gather my notes and vacate the front desk so he can take over.

As he accepts a greeting from Skye by scratching behind her pointy ears, he asks, "So, what happened to your receptionist?"

I back toward my office, hating that I have to go through the whole embarrassing story again. "I, um… lost him."

"You lost him? Like he's missing?"

"He's not a missing person. He's just missing from this office and my life."

My breezy delivery of this is apparently not enough for my old buddy. "Explain."

After I give him the quick and dirty story of my weekend, he just shakes his head. "You have got to start putting as much effort into choosing boyfriends as you do the rest of your life."

"So everyone keeps telling me. But I also remember y'all calling me a fuddy-duddy because I was too much of a control freak back in the day, so how about you give me a break?"

"Speaking of which, I'm kind of surprised you actually quit your teaching job to do this. What happened? Found out you didn't like kids after all?"

"I loved the kids. Still do. It was the parents and the bureaucracy that drove me nuts. While getting paid less than I made working the front desk at the Rumrunner Hotel."

He leans back in the desk chair. "So it's about the money?"

"It is more money, but honestly?" I gesture around the small suite of offices. "This is my dream job. Better yet, I don't have to leave town to do it."

My grandparents had all the same questions when I made this decision, so I'm ready with answers. "Running around signing up extras is one thing, but last summer, when I contracted with Jay Fowler and his dad to run day-player auditions, I was actually using my entire skill set. Now that they've outsourced *all* the local casting for an entire season of a network TV show to me, I can hire all the actors I've been directing over the years. Even kids I taught at the high school and in my Saturday classes. Plus, I'm getting good feedback," I add with pride. "The director on the first two episodes of *Lawson's* said he didn't think he'd be able to use regional talent, but he was impressed with the people I found."

"But are there enough shows to work here year-round? I thought the sound stages were empty half the time."

I perch on the edge of the desk. This is my chance to convince Ford that he'd be better off staying versus going back to LA. "The state's tax incentives plus the fact that we've got good local crews has really made Wallington's reputation. They're calling it the Hollywood of the East."

"Seriously?"

"*Lawson's Reach* will be shooting for nine months. So on top of the indie films and TV movies, there's plenty of work. That's why it made sense for me to lease this office for the whole year."

"How's that?"

"The rent is half as much if I do a whole year instead of month-to-month. I put a big chunk of my savings into the video camera and lights and the VCRs, but I'll build that back up in no time." I gesture through the open door to my office to the shelves lining its walls, each one full to bursting with crates of background casting cards and actor headshots. "Best of all, I don't have to move everything from the garage every time I start a new project."

The phone rings, reminding me that I need to get to my desk. Hoping that I've given Ford some food for thought, I hop up to head into my office. "In the meantime, I appreciate *you* playing the role of receptionist for the day."

Blessedly, he drops his feet to the ground and picks up the ringing phone without giving me any more grief. By the time I sit behind my own desk, Skye has curled up on the floor next to him.

Good girl. Even she's in on convincing him to stay. Ford always did want a dog.

Dialing my brain back to work mode, I prioritize tasks on my to-do list as I sip my now-cold coffee. At the top I write, *Find a new assistant who isn't an actor.* "Or a cute younger guy," I murmur, reminded of the cute younger guy occupying the office next door. Before I can get lost in musings about what exactly he's doing over there—production accounting, maybe, or union rep—I school my mind back to the tasks at hand.

I have a slate of actresses coming in this afternoon for a small speaking role in the third episode of *Lawson's Reach*, I have auditions tomorrow for a Santa role in a Hallmark Hall of Fame movie shooting next month, and I've got to finalize things for the thirty-some-odd extras I need to show up at the beach tomorrow for a low-budget indie film.

Checking my notes, I'm happy to find that it's shooting right next to the Rumrunner Hotel. Where Nate is staying. I'm lost in a replay of some of the best moments from last night's episode when Skye barks sharply, startling me into spilling the remains of my coffee onto my list. "Shit."

"Sorry, Vi," Ford says from the doorway. "But Jay's on the phone. He says it's important."

CHAPTER 4

LAWSON'S REACH "PILOT"

FOR THE NEW KID, THINGS AREN'T AS PEACHY AS THEY'D SEEMED IN THE PEACEFUL COASTAL TOWN.

NATE

IT'S NOT EVEN 7:00 A.M. IN LA, AND MY SISTER IS LIKELY IN THE process of getting her kids out the door to school, but this can't wait. Her husband answers the phone, but when I tell him it's an emergency, he hands me over to her.

"This better be a real emergency and not a casting emergency," Monica says. "Sweetie, you have to wear pants to school. It's a rule. What do you want?"

It takes a beat for me to realize that the question is directed at me, and not my nephew, who decided recently that pants are an unnecessary encumbrance. I'm not one for small talk and she's busy, so I get right to it. "Are we poaching here? Did you know there's already a casting office in town?"

"What do you mean?"

"I've got production expecting tape from me, but I just got

off the phone with an agent who says she has people going in to read for *Lawson's Reach*. Today. For the casting director next door."

"Oh my fucking god. Shit. Sorry, sweetie. Yep, that's two quarters for the swear jar."

"What am I supposed to do? Go next door and say, 'Sorry, lady, but can you send those actors over here this afternoon?'"

"I'm going to kill dad. Oh, don't cry, sweetie. I'm not really going to kill Grandpa. That would be illegal."

"Do I have to call him?" My dad and I don't get along even when things are going well.

She lets out the martyred sigh Jewish mothers young and old somehow master by the time their kids are old enough to get in trouble. "No, I'll do it."

"I guess I can go next door and see if it isn't just some sort of mix-up."

"That would be good. Hopefully, that's all it is. But you know how he and Uncle Rob are."

Before I can ask what exactly she means by that, she says, "Gotta go. I'm out of quarters for the swear jar. Call me on the car phone when you've got the 411."

VIOLET

"He's on line three," Ford says before going back to the front desk. "Before you take it, is it okay if I grab some lunch? I'll just walk over to catering. I'll take Skye out too."

"Damn," I stand to stretch my stiff limbs. And a few places that got an extra workout last night. "Where did the morning go?"

"Where it always does. You want something?"

I nod gratefully and ask him to get me whatever he's having, even though something tells me this phone call will erase my appetite. Only way out is through, however, so I sit back down and punch the little blinking button. "What's up, Jay?"

"I don't know what happened," Jay starts right in without a greeting. "But something did, and I have a good idea who's behind it."

"I need a little more information here, Jay. I've got extras to call and a session this afternoon."

"Not anymore you don't. Session's canceled."

"What? Why? Did they do another rewrite?"

"I don't have any idea. All I know is we no longer have the local casting for *Lawson's Reach*."

It's a good thing I was already sitting because otherwise I'd be flat on my ass. "What? How can they do that? Don't we have a contract or something?"

"That's one of many questions I have. Only thing I can come up with is—" He breaks off and clears his throat. "They didn't use any local actors for the pilot last year, right? Just extras."

"That's correct as far as I know."

"Who hired you to do the background casting? Was it a casting director?"

"No, I worked directly with the network production company on that."

"Well, when the pilot got picked up, we managed to get the contract for locals and extras, but if whoever's doing the top-of-show casting had a problem with that, they might have put up a fuss. Especially if it's who I think it is."

My heart rate picked up the moment I heard the word canceled, but now it skips a beat. I'd had a strange phone call with an LA casting director promising me regular work if *I* promised to never work with the Fowlers again. Figuring the guy was some sort of crank, I told him to fuck off. Could that person with a vendetta against Jay and his family have something to do with this?

"Jay, this show was the main reason why I set up shop full-time. If that's not happening, are you going to have other work to throw my way?"

"Honestly, I don't know."

"But I—"

"I know. You quit your job."

"The job with benefits and a pension."

"The job you hated," he reminds me.

"I'm sure I'll hate being unemployed even more."

"Let's not panic just yet. Like I said, I think I know who snagged this out from under us, and if I'm right—Oh, hang on a sec, Vi. I've got another call coming in that might give me some answers. Be right back."

Music from Jay's favorite Boston radio station fills my ears. WBAR's lineup is better than your usual hold music, but I'm too agitated to enjoy it. The phone cord stretches behind me as I cross my office to examine the wall calendar that represents the next couple of months of my life. Represen*ted*. Erasing a new episode of *Lawson's Reach* every ten days will leave me with just a commercial here, a TV movie there. Which won't bring in enough to cover my office rent and living expenses. Not to mention hiring anyone else.

Guess it's a good thing Lance left.

"Just as I suspected," Jay blurts in my ear, startling me. "It's my damn uncle's company. They cast the pilot, and he managed to guilt production into reverting local casting back to him. He sent my cousin Nate to open an office in Wallington, and they're calling it—get this—Carolina Casting."

"But I searched the state records. Someone already registered an LLC with that name."

"Either they bought it from someone else or created the company before last fall. I wouldn't put it past Alan Fowler to register LLCs all over the country to get ahead of the game."

The name "Nate" echoes in my mind as I struggle to wrap

38

my mind around this news. "Wait, you said your cousin's name is Nate? And he's here?"

"Yep. Flew in from LA."

"Does he happen to look like Dylan McDermott?"

"Uh, sorta? I think he's more of a Dermot Mulroney. Why?"

It all drops into place. "I met him. Last night. At the Rumrunner. He's a guest there. The office they opened is right next door."

And it seems I may have slept with the enemy.

NATE

When I crack open the front door to Casting Carolina, it's clear that, despite the artwork on its logo, this place has got nothing to do with fishing. Framed movie posters—most of them autographed—decorate the walls of the outer office. There's a small table by the door with a Screen Actors Guild sign-in sheet, just like there is at every single legit casting office in New York or LA.

There's a crate on the front desk, and I can see from the doorway that it's filled to the brim with the info cards used to keep track of all the pertinent details needed to cast background actors—height, weight, age, race, yada yada yada—stapled to a Polaroid photo of the actor.

No one's growling at me yet, so either her dog isn't here anymore or it didn't hear me come in, and she hasn't noticed my entrance either. In fact, I can see her through the window to an interior office, hair up in a messy bun that looks like it's held up by two pencils, talking on the phone. The cord is pulled tight across the room, and the phone itself teeters dangerously on the edge of the desk. She's got a pen in her mouth, and she's making Xs on the calendar with a bright red marker.

Sunlight glints on her hair, bringing out more shades of coppery red than I can count. A memory from last night flashes through my mind: that hair spread out across the pillow, her eyes closed in bliss, the creamy skin of her cheek flushed with pleasure. Pleasure that I made her feel.

But when she turns and catches me standing in the doorway, it's clear she is not happy to see me now.

VIOLET

Since Ford took Skye with him to lunch, I get no warning when Nate shows up in my office doorway, maddeningly gorgeous even with a guilty look on his face.

"Um, can I talk to you?" he asks. "I think we might have a problem."

Before he can launch into whatever lame explanation he's got for yanking a full season of prime-time casting out from under me, I fire first. "Am I just extra lucky?"

His brows furrow like he's confused, but I just keep pounding. "Do you always seduce a woman after you rob her blind? Or was that a pity fuck?"

"I mean, to set the record straight," he says, "I think you were the one who was doing the seducing."

"You could've stopped me in that parking lot. Told me you were swooping in from the big city to take everything I've worked so hard for."

Hands up defensively, he says, "I had no idea you were a casting director."

"What about this morning? When you saw the fucking sign on my door?"

"I thought you sold fishing supplies. There's a rod and reel on that sign."

"Fishing supplies? On a studio lot?"

I knew I should've made Sully's cousin redo that sign, but I didn't have the heart. He worked so hard, and it's so pretty. He just didn't think to ask me what business I was in, and I didn't think to tell him.

Wiping that aside, I find another vein of attack. "Don't you think it's a bit shady to take over casting a show that's already in production? One that I've got actors coming in to audition for in less than an hour?"

"Are you sure that's what has happened? That there wasn't some sort of mix-up?"

"Is your name Nate Fowler?"

He grimaces. "It is."

"Well, Nate Fowler, your cousin Jay just filled me in on what sounds more like highway robbery than a mix-up." I tick off the series of events on my fingers. "Your family's company did the *Lawson's Reach* pilot. Jay's family's company got the series. Then your father managed to talk the network into reneging on that deal, y'all have the show again, and I may be going out of business." I turn away, kicking a wastebasket out of the way in hopes that it'll cover the tears coloring my voice. "Too bad I quit my fucking job."

"What job?"

"I was a high school drama teacher who only did casting in the summer. Until this summer, when I *thought* I had nine months of guaranteed work."

"Look, I'll do my best to..." He scrubs a hand over his face without finishing his sentence.

I want to punch something, but I settle for throwing a magic marker across the room. "What about the actresses coming in to read this afternoon? Some of them drive hours to get here. It's too late to cancel."

"They drive hours for a role with only a line or two?"

41

"Actors drive from as far as Virginia, Atlanta, and even Miami for a chance to get union work. Something you'll have to pick up on pretty darn quick." Crossing my arms over my chest, I tip my chin up. "So, what do I tell them?"

"Well, maybe we could pay you for the time you spent arranging the auditions, and you can just send them next door?"

Even though my gut tells me that Nate probably wasn't manipulating me last night, it's still tough to take that this rich daddy's boy has my dream job. "You've got balls, mister. I'll give you that."

Seems I've painted myself into a corner. I have to accept his offer, or the actors will suffer. That doesn't stop me from hurling more venom at him, though. "Anything else I can do to make things easier for you?" I grab my Rolodex and flip through it. "Why don't I just hand this over to you? You could copy all the contacts I've spent the last few years collecting."

I fling my arm toward the filing cabinets and stacks of submissions on the shelves in my office. "You may as well just ransack the place. None of this will do me any good now."

He opens his mouth like he's going to… I don't know what. Tears threaten behind my eyes—of rage, frustration, grief, and who knows what all—none of which I want this man to see.

I march to the door and open it wide. "You need to leave. I'll put up a sign telling the actors for today's session to go next door. Consider it an office-warming gift."

He backs up, one step and then another, but it's not fast enough.

"What the hell are you waiting for? Get. Out."

After slamming my door behind him I shout, "And don't ever darken my door again!"

NATE

Back in my own office, I'm trying to decide whether to go straight to the top or get my sister's perspective before calling my dad, when the phone rings.

"Carolina Casting." Words I'd been so proud to say just an hour ago sour in my mouth. When I was totally hyped for this opportunity to flex my own muscles in this business, to prove to my family that I bring something to the table. Now I wish I were back in Ohio making sure employees are happy while they get widget A from point B to point C with the least amount of friction.

"What did you find out?" my sister asks without preamble.

"Did we do the casting for the pilot of *Lawson's Reach*?"

"We did, but from here. We did hire a girl down there to do extras, but that was pretty simple, just a bunch of kids to be high schoolers. The front lawn, a couple classrooms, changing classes in the halls. Easy stuff."

"Well, I guess that *girl* opened a permanent casting office here, with the promise from Uncle Rob and Jay that she'd be doing the local casting on *Lawson's Reach* for the entire season. She's got auditions for it today."

"I mean, that's unfortunate, but it sounds like Rob took a show that should've been ours."

"Doesn't Fowler Stern usually stay away from the East Coast, though? Like the two brothers had an agreement to divide the country at the Mississippi River or something?"

"I don't think there was ever any agreement. There was a *dis*agreement, and then Uncle Rob and Daddy never spoke to each other again."

"Yeah, well, I'm getting the feeling that sending me here is less about business and more about Uncle Jay and Dad. What the heck is their problem, anyway?"

She takes a long sip of something, probably the sweet

coffee drink she's been addicted to ever since Starbucks opened a drive-through in Beverly Hills. "You were just a toddler. There was a big screaming match at our grandma's funeral."

"About what?"

"About her. Actually, both their mom and their dad. I didn't really understand it at the time, but I found this giant file in Dad's office a couple of years ago when I was looking for something else. It was all these newspaper clippings. Every interview where an actor or producer or director said something nice about him, but also when someone said something critical. When I asked him about the file, he pointed at the stack of critical quotes and blamed them all on Uncle Rob."

"That seems a little paranoid."

"Apparently, Rob gave an interview right before the funeral. He claimed that he was the rightful heir to the so-called casting dynasty because the business their parents started in New York only hires what he called 'real' actors."

I can hear the air quotes from two thousand miles away.

"I don't know if you know this," she continues, "But when their parents got divorced, Dad and Grandpa moved to LA to open the office here. Meanwhile, Uncle Rob stayed with Grandma. He worked for her and so did his wife. They all say that the California office is a cheap copy of the original because we only cast pretty boys and girls who can't act their way out of a paper bag."

"Isn't that kind of the truth?"

"No. Well, I mean, sometimes. But we've done some movies where people won awards, and it wasn't for their looks."

"Well, right now it sucks that Violet's in the middle of it."

"Who is Violet?"

"She's the local casting director. The one that does background. I mean, this'll destroy her brand-new business."

"Maybe she shouldn't have started it up without a firmer deal."

"That's a little—"

"You know," she says, interrupting me. "We still need someone to do background. And if we pick up another show or two, you'll need help. You could hire her."

"Away from Jay and Rob. That'd make Dad happy."

"Two birds with one stone, baby." A beep sounds, and then a click. "Ugh, Adam's calling. I guess I'll have to take it."

"Wow. You're talking about Adam, your husband, right? You couldn't be a little more enthusiastic?"

"You want some relationship advice?"

I don't think anyone in my family is in a position to give out relationship advice. Monica and her husband bicker constantly, my mom is about to have a "commitment ceremony" with her latest wacked-out herbalist/healer/guru, and my dad has been married four times. Pretty sure his current girlfriend is younger than I am. And me? I can't seem to stay in one place long enough to get attached.

Despite the fact that I didn't say yea or nay, my sister's going on and on about how you should never get into a workplace power dynamic with your spouse.

"I mean, I can't push to cast him in every damn project. Plus, I need him to be around for the kids."

"Have you told him that?"

"Not in those words."

"Maybe a little honesty is in order."

"Honesty is dangerous, little brother." Her bark of a laugh is caustic. "Gotta go. Glad this got sorted."

Before I can argue that it's hardly sorted, she's gone.

VIOLET

That evening, I'm at the table in the kitchen of my grandparents' inn going over projected income and expenses sans *Lawson's Reach* and coming up with a negative balance, when the cup of tea I've let go cold gets whisked away. Before I know it, a full glass of wine lands in its place, and my grandmother sits down next to me.

I'm so embarrassed by the spot I've gotten myself into I can't quite make myself look at her.

"What happened, sweetheart? You're starting to worry me."

The last thing my grandparents need is to add me to their list of concerns, which already includes an antique Victorian inn and their own aging bodies, so I paste on a smile and force myself to lift the glass. "Nothing important."

"Don't bullshit me, young lady."

Her choice of words is so surprising that the wine goes down the wrong pipe. After I clear the pathway, I rasp. "Gran!"

"Big lies call for big words."

After she stares at me, unblinking, for a full minute, I finally spit it out. "I messed up."

Despite the shrug I add to my admission, her brows crawl even further up her forehead. "At work. I should never have left my teaching job. I obviously don't know how to run a business."

"Well, now that seems unlikely. You've been very successful at the casting business."

"I was. Until I got royally screwed over—I mean, until I got in the middle of a family feud."

"My word. What does a family feud have to do with it?"

I tell her the whole story, minus the part about me sleeping with Nate. My grandparents are very liberal and don't expect me to be a virgin until I'm married or anything, but I don't exactly chat about sex with my grandma like I'm Carrie and she's Samantha.

When I'm finished, she pats my hand. "Did I ever tell you about the huge mistake we made the first summer after we bought the inn?"

"Um, no?" They bought the inn after my grandpa retired from the Coast Guard fifteen years ago. I was thirteen and didn't really pay attention to anything but the dramas of being in junior high.

She sits back in her chair and looks out the window. "We had no business buying this old gal. When we opened, we didn't have any systems in place. We just thought it would be fun to have people stay. Looking back at it now, I can't believe the bank approved the mortgage."

"Was that the mistake? Taking out the loan?"

"Oh, no. That was fine. What happened was, your grand-father and I had different methods for taking reservations. Whoever answered the phone would write down the reserva-tion in a calendar. Unfortunately, it wasn't the same calendar."

"Uh-oh."

My grandmother shakes her head, but she's laughing. "Memorial Day weekend we opened our doors, and we had twice as many guests as we had beds."

"Oh my god! What did you do?"

"We begged forgiveness from everyone, called all of our friends who had guest rooms until we found everyone a place to stay, and then we threw a huge party."

"Were people mad?"

"One couple was upset. But we explained that it was a simple, if stupid, mistake. In the end, people had so much fun every single one of those guests has returned again and again."

A memory surfaces. "Is that why I had to go stay with Dani that weekend?"

She laughs again. "That is correct. I needed your room."

As she often does, Gran has put a smile on my face, but it doesn't last. "I've got the opposite problem. And I'm worried that the whole local actor community will suffer if I don't just roll over and give all my contacts to this other company."

"That seems a bit extreme." She purses her lips for a moment. "You may be new at running a business, but from what I've seen, you've spent the past few summers building up a résumé. I don't think you should give in just yet. Sometimes you have to shake the trees to get the fruit to fall. In the meantime, we won't kick you to the curb if you can't pay rent."

"I don't pay rent, Gran."

"You do in labor."

I wave that down. "I'm just helping out."

"Exactly. We help each other out. That's what family does."

Unless you're my parents, of course. Then you disappear.

CHAPTER 5

NATE

THE ONLY PLACE I'VE EVER BEEN ABLE TO FIND PEACE IS ON THE water. After my parents' divorce, my mom moved us from Beverly Hills to Topanga, where she could fully embrace her hippie side. A teenager at the time, my sister despised living in the canyon. Her favorite words for the place were *lame*, *heinous*, and *bogus*. But I loved waking up surrounded by woods and wildlife instead of concrete and traffic. Best of all, the ocean was less than a mile away. The first time I successfully popped up and found the edge that let me carve a route from break to shore, I was hooked on surfing. It was the only power I had, the only time I felt like I could harness the chaos around me and literally keep my head above water. Even when I'd fail and get pounded by the waves, I could just go at it again.

After a day like yesterday—one clusterfuck after another, all created by my father's damn ego—I need that perspective.

Problem is, it's tourist season. If I wait until the shops are open so I can rent a board, I'll not only be late for work, the waves will be crowded with swimmers and waders.

Deciding to just go for a swim, I jog up the beach to the pier where I've seen surfers gather the past two mornings, figuring I can at least gather some intel.

When I arrive, a dozen bodies dot the water's surface in a dawn patrol, lined up just beyond the break. The sun isn't far from the horizon, but the air is heating up quickly.

Dropping the towel I brought from my room and pulling off my shirt, I begin to jog toward the water when a male voice calls, "Hey, man, you don't want to swim there. You'll run into traffic before you know it."

When I turn around, I'm unprepared for the size of the guy. He's got a board under his arm, but he's not built like your typical surfer. Instead of a long, lean frame, he's broad enough to be a linebacker. Or with the beard he's sporting, maybe a lumberjack. Despite his intimidating size, his smile is welcoming.

"I don't know what I was thinking." I shake my head and gesture towards the water. "I'm so used to having my board with me, I guess I forgot what I was doing for a minute there."

"What happened to your board?" the guy asks, the level of concern in his voice almost comical.

"Nothing, it's just back home in LA. I'm here for work and didn't realize I might need one."

He nods slowly, "Didn't think there'd be waves to ride, you mean."

I grin. "Maybe. We Californians tend to be a bit snobby."

"A bit?" He snorts. "I grew up on this water. Then I spent the last seven years in SoCal."

"And?"

He juts his chin at the water. "I'll take the Atlantic any day."

When he winces, I follow his gaze. At the crest of a wave, a girl pearls, and her tail rockets up.

"Whoops," my companion says.

"It happens," I say with a shrug. "I hope I can get out there myself. Any recommendations for a good place to rent a board?"

"Puh." He punches his own board into the sand and then begins to walk toward the dunes. When I don't follow, he turns back with a beckoning wave. "Come on. You can borrow one of mine."

"Seriously? You don't even know my name."

He sticks out his hand. "What's your name, friend?"

Shaking his meaty hand, I can't help but mirror his grin. "Nate."

"Sully. Welcome to Carolina."

VIOLET

It's hard to believe that less than twenty-four hours ago I was hoping to run into Nate while I checked in background actors for the B-movie shooting down at the beach. Now, I'm wishing he'd just disappear.

Or that things were different.

Due to some miscalculation, my grandpa didn't make enough breakfast for the guests, let alone me, so after I get my people situated, I stop by the catering truck to pick up a sausage and egg biscuit before driving back to the studio. I'm also thinking that hanging out with the crew of this show could be a way to shake the tree, as Gran suggested. Someone's got to have a line on what's coming into town next. If I can get a jump on Nate and reach out to a producer directly, maybe I can add some work back onto my schedule.

After I go through the line, Whitney waves to me from a

table under the tent. The rest of the hair and makeup crew is already throwing their trash away and heading for their respective trailers, but Whit calls that she'll be with them shortly and pats the seat next to her.

The moment my butt hits the folding chair she says, "Oh, honey, I'm so sorry."

"What's going on?" I ask, wondering what she knows that I don't.

"I heard about the rival casting office that set up right next door."

"What? That just happened yesterday." Hair and makeup is gossip central, but this news traveled faster than usual. "How did you hear?"

She tips her head to the side as she recalls the sequence of events. "A guy we had in yesterday is friends with a girl who was supposed to read for you but had to go next door and audition with… what's his name?"

"Nate."

"Nate. That's right." She nods but quickly shifts to a shake of the head. "Wait—it wasn't the same Nate that we were talking to Sunday night, was it?"

"Strangely enough, it was." Whit, like all of my friends, can read me like a book, so I take a big bite of my biscuit in an attempt to hide the fact that just the thought of Nate riles me up in more ways than one.

"I guess he wasn't a traveling salesman or a pharmaceutical rep, then."

"Mm-hmph."

"Well, apparently, he's no you," she says. Thankfully, she's pulled out her compact to powder her nose and reapply lipstick as she shares the intel, so her attention's off of me. "He rushed through her audition, didn't give the girl any notes, didn't even try to act when he read the lines with her. Her friend said she was really upset. She was so thrown she's sure she lost any chance at the job."

I was pissed off before, but now I'm fit to be tied. It's one thing for *me* to get screwed, another for the actors in our community to lose work because of him.

"What the heck happened?" Whitney prods.

"I'm not actually sure. Something to do with a family feud between Jay Fowler and this guy Nate. Or, rather, their parents. Brothers who are using me and my business as a way to get back at each other."

"I'm so sorry," Whitney says, patting my arm. "Anything I can do to help? Slash his tires? Firebomb his house?"

Whitney is 5'2" and as tiny as a mite. That, on top of the sweet tone with which she makes these suggestions has me laughing. "I appreciate your enthusiasm, but I'd like to stay on the right side of the law."

"You know my family has all kinds of connections."

Never sure whether to take what she says seriously, I press on. "If I'm going to survive, I'm going to have to lobby for everything and anything that comes into town. If you can keep your ear to the ground and let me know what you hear, that'd be awesome."

She claps delightedly. "Finally, my gossip skills will be of use!"

"It's not your fault that you make people comfortable when you do their hair and makeup."

She shrugs. "True. They just can't help but tell me all."

"Exactly."

"And I do try and use my powers for good rather than evil. It's too bad Ford and Sully aren't working right now," she says, tapping her chin with her finger. As usual her nails are painted to match her outfit. "I mean, I hear juicy stuff from the actors, but the sound cart is where the suits hang out. Then you'd get more of the 411 on what new shows are coming into town."

"Speaking of which, how is all that going?"

"All what?"

"I mean, are things okay between the three of you?"

"I don't see them outside of the group. I'm too busy." She waves a hand in the air vaguely.

"You haven't exactly moved on, though."

"Just because I've been able to resist every dipshit developer or randy real estate attorney my parents try to match me up with? That has more to do with not wanting to play their game. You are so lucky your parents aren't around to monitor your every move."

My parents dropped me with my grandparents when I was five and only come home for major holidays. If that. When I think of them, it's mostly with resentment. "I guess I never really thought about it that way."

"Dani's the lucky one," Whitney says. "Has her own place and just hangs out with the 'rents when she feels like it.

"You have your own place."

"No, I have *Dani's* place. But it's better than living at home."

"Couldn't you afford your own place? I thought you just lived with her to keep her cousins from filling the void."

"There is that. But I couldn't pay for a one-bedroom and still afford all the things that make me beautiful." She says this with a dazzling, if slightly jaded, smile.

I take her hand. "Whit, I hope you don't really think that. You'd be gorgeous even if you cut your hair with nail clippers and wore sky-blue eyeshadow."

Predictably, she gasps like I've uttered a complete and total heresy. "Hush your mouth."

"Seriously, though. You could spend a little less on products and fashion and still look better than ninety percent of the population."

She tips her head to the side again. "Where does all your money go? You don't pay any rent."

"I couldn't have afforded to sign a year's lease for my

office if I was also spending money on an apartment. As it is, I might not be able to afford the lease at all."

"We really need to find you more work."

"Exactly."

"Good thing Lance left so you don't have to pay him." She bumps shoulders with me. "He wasn't good enough for you anyway, you know."

I rest my chin on my hand as I look out over the beach. The Rumrunner is just down the street. The place where I got the note from Lance before meeting Nate. "He was kind of boring, especially compared to—" *Oops. Didn't mean to go there.*

"Compared to who?"

"Nothing. Nobody, I mean."

She narrows her eyes at me. "Wait a minute. Did something happen between you and your rival after he walked you to your car the other night?"

I get up and throw away my trash, but she follows me. "Did it?"

"Maybe," I say to the trash can.

"I reckon that makes things a bit more complicated."

"If it happens again. Which it won't."

She goes back to the table to gather her things. "Maybe if it did, you could seduce him into giving up."

I shrug, a rare swell of pessimism swamping me. "And then he'd leave town."

"Are you afraid you'd fall for him? Was the sex that good?"

I sigh. "It was pretty mind-blowing. And difficult to stop thinking about."

"You need something to look forward to." She hooks her arm in mine and steers me away from the catering truck. "How about a trip to Masonboro this weekend?"

Even the thought of an afternoon on the beach that few tourists know about perks me right up. "We'd need a boat.

Sully's sailboat would get us across the intracoastal, but it'd be a pain in the butt."

"It'd work in a pinch, but I think I can rustle up a skiff. Leave it to me."

When we get to the makeup trailer, I give her a hug. "Love you, girl."

"Love you too, Vi," she echoes with a squeeze. Stepping out of my embrace, she pats me on the arm. "It'll work out, you'll see. We'll all help. You're like the mayor of all the actors in town. In the state, practically. Everyone will rally around you."

As I walk back to my car, I mull over her words of encouragement. Problem is, even if she's right about how people feel, actors aren't the ones with the power. They have to go wherever the work is being offered. And I can't blame them for that.

I should never have started a business based on that promise from Jay. Someday I'll learn the lesson that I can't rely on anyone but myself.

You'd think my parents would've taught me that already.

NATE

After an hour on the water, I've got my head on straight again. Driving into the office down winding roads flanked by gorgeous marshes and wild forest is an added balm. There's something about Wallington that makes me feel like I'd actually want to stay a while.

I've never felt like I quite fit in anywhere I've lived. Bouncing back and forth between my mom's hippy-dippy neighborhood in Topanga and my dad's in class-conscious Beverly Hills, my roots in both places were shallow. I went to three colleges in three different towns, and I've had six jobs in six different places in the four years since graduation. I'm an expert at moving, but I've got zero experience settling in anywhere.

It's only been a few days, but I have to say, in this place—something between a town and a city, where water is everywhere you look—the rhythm feels right. There's litter on the beaches, but that's a problem everywhere. No traffic, though, and the people are friendly.

Except for one person. She's summed up what's between us, and I'm not on the plus side.

I don't blame her, but despite making an effort to give her space, I can't seem to stay away from her. Even now, as I walk down the hall of the production building, I keep my gaze forward as I pass by Casting Carolina. This time, it's not the scent of freesias that catches my attention, but a loud "Ho, ho, ho!"

It's only when I've got my hand on the doorknob to my office that I clock what I saw inside hers. It's so odd, I retrace my steps and peer around the door frame to make sure I wasn't imagining things.

No Violet or growling dog in sight. Instead, nine men occupy the front room. Eight of them are in full-on Santa suits —red coat, black belt, white beard, the whole nine yards. The ninth man does not belong in the Santa set. Tall, lean, and broad-shouldered, the guy looks like every wannabe leading man that ever entered our offices back in Beverly Hills. With his longish blond hair and ice-blue eyes, he could grace the cover of any fan magazine.

Guess Violet's found herself another boy toy. The bitterly jealous tone echoing inside my head tells me that I am not happy about the new development.

"Can I help you?" Not-Santa asks. Before I can answer, he looks me up and down and then flips through the stack of headshots on his clipboard. "I'm pretty sure we're not seeing businessmen until tomorrow. Did you make an appointment for this morning?"

It takes me a beat to realize that he thinks I'm an actor. "No, I'm… I work next door."

His welcoming smile flattens into a grim line. "You're the Carolina Casting guy."

I hold out my hand anyway. "I'm Nate."

After a long beat he shakes it, his grip firm but not crushing. "Ford."

"Do you… work here?" I ask, not sure what I want the answer to be.

"Nah, I'm just helping Vi out. She's one of my best friends." He looks at me long and hard. "And I don't like seeing people mess with her."

Unsure whether he's referring to the fact that we slept together or the family feud that's affecting her business, or both, I just nod. "It's not my intention to hurt her."

"But you have."

"It seems so."

"Maybe you need to make it your intention to *help* her. To make up for"—he waves a hand back and forth in the air—"whatever happened."

"Is she here?"

"Not yet. She had to check in extras down at the beach this morning, and then she's picking up some kids at the Boys and Girls Clubs to take them to a set downtown."

"She's driving extras to work? Child extras?" When he nods, I add, "Why the hell is she doing that?"

"Because that's the only way they'll get there. Not everyone has a car in this town."

Before I can protest that the practice seems way out of her job description, as well as a legal nightmare, one of the Santas calls out, "Ford, I need to be back in Myrtle Beach by noon. When we goin' to get this party started?"

"Just waitin' on the boss lady," Ford answers. "I'm sure she'll be back any minute. Everybody got their sides?"

The dude couldn't be nicer to the herd of cranky old Santas. I don't envy him, and I for sure can't help, so I make my exit.

"Nice to meet you, Nate. Welcome to Wallington."

The thing I'm finding about Southerners? Maybe it's me, but when everything they say is laced with that sweet tone, it's hard to read the subtext. "Welcome to Wallington" could mean anything from "We're so happy you're here" to—and I think this is the case with Ford—"Watch your step, buddy, because if you fuck with my friend, I will make you regret it."

CHAPTER 6

Lawson's Reach, "Kiss"

When the class movie hits a speed bump, Lawson gains an advantage.

VIOLET

This situation is killing me. Not only am I worried about my own financial future, but for the past three days there's been a steady stream of actors stopping by with their sob stories. Just now, an actor I've directed in multiple theater roles over the years told me he was worried he screwed up his audition because Nate was so intimidating.

I gave him my best talking-to, reminding him that he's got to be "director-proof," that he can't rely on anyone but himself to ensure his performance is top-notch. He's got to have the technique to get there on his own.

I feel bad for the guy, but there isn't a damn thing I can do about it. Except get on the phone to try and drum up work.

After three calls to New York and Los Angeles production companies I've contracted with in the past to let each one know that I'm available and ready to find them day players now, as well as extras, I decide to visit craft services for a snack. Maybe the fortification of caffeine and sugar will give me the energy I need to tour the stages and beg for work.

When I round the corner of the closest soundstage, I find that my neighbor has had the same idea. Before I can slink away, however, Randy shouts my name.

"Hey there, Violet. I've got those turtle brownies you love today."

Well, shit. Not only can I not resist that combo of chocolate and caramel and nuts—which add protein, you know—it'd be rude to ignore him.

As I approach, Nate's expression comes into focus. Regret is written all over his face. Question is, what does he regret? Sleeping with me? Ruining my life? Or both?

Determined not to let Nate run my entire world, I turn my flirtiest smile on Randy. He's the one offering me mood-enhancing chocolate, after all. "You are the devil, Randy. You know I can't resist you."

Sex with Nate packed more of a serotonin boost than the darkest chocolate, but we are not thinking about that right now. At least not in our waking hours. Still, I can't help but enjoy the frown my words and tone put on Nate's face.

"I see you've met my new rival, Randy."

"Rival?" Randy says, his bushy brows coming together. "I thought y'all were working together."

"Oh, no. Nate's company swooped in from the big city and snatched that new show away from me." Hand to heaving bosom, I play up the tragic heroine, hopefully not overdoing it. "But you know me, Randy. I will survive."

My performance lands, apparently, because Randy stops pouring and hands Nate a half-filled cup of coffee.

Hand on Nate's arm—resisting the powerful urge to run it up and down to feel those muscles again—I give him a treacly smile. "We're so lucky that Randy keeps us fed and watered. He certainly doesn't have to since we're not officially cast or crew members. But since there's nowhere else to get lunch or even a decent cup of coffee way out here"—we're only ten minutes from downtown, but even that's a pain in the butt to get to when you're working a twelve-hour day—"I think I'd starve or my head would explode from lack of caffeine without him."

Randy shakes his head. "What they serve at the service station shouldn't even be called the same thing. That's not coffee, it's water stained brown."

"Bless you and your culinary skills, Randy. This brownie is going to get me through an afternoon of trying my best to scrounge up a few jobs so I can pay my rent. You'll let me know if you hear anything about new shows coming to town?"

"I sure will, honey. And you take another brownie for later, Vi. And a cup of coffee." He pours me a large cup, adding cream and sugar the way he knows I like it.

"You're the best, Randy," I say on an adoring sigh. "See you tomorrow."

Even taking the longest strides I can in my espadrille wedges, Nate catches up to me before I can make it back inside my office.

"I guess I deserved that."

"That and more." Without an audience, there's no need to hide how I really feel, so I whirl to face him. "I've spent the morning *looking* for work instead of *doing* the work. Meanwhile, I'm hearing complaints from actors that your readings are so wooden their auditions are suffering."

He frowns in response to my tirade, but it somehow adds to his allure, which makes me madder than a wet hen. "You swanning in here is not just bad for me, it's bad for them. If you can't figure out how to run an audition, you'll damage the reputation of everyone in this community. We've worked hard to convince the powers-that-be that we've got crews and performers that are just as good as the ones you've got out west, despite the 'we know better' attitudes every single director and producer brings with them. We're not just pretty scenery here, you know—we're professionals."

I step into his space, but instead of backing off, he meets me halfway. Shaking with an unnerving combination of desire and fury, I poke a finger at his chest. "If you fuck that up, I will…"

Suddenly, I can't rightly remember what it is I can or will or may do, because I'm falling headfirst into the dark pool of his heated gaze. His mouth opens, probably to argue with me, and it takes every bit of will in me to keep from dragging a finger across those soft, firm lips. My needy breasts are millimeters away from pressing themselves to his rock-hard pecs. The only words that could possibly come out of my mouth in this moment would beg him to run his hands over every inch of my electrified skin.

A door slams, startling me out of a daze of pure lust.

And then I run away.

NATE

I make it to my office without exploding, even though I'm racked with a raging need to take that woman up against any and every surface of this office or her office or even a picnic table outside. Or the back of my car. I've never felt this turned on, this out of my mind with desire for anyone.

I may have come here to prove myself, but I'm not leaving without making things right for Violet. Fuck my dad and my uncle and their stupid feud. She's right. They're messing with other people's livelihoods.

I don't want to endure the inevitable discomfort that calling my dad on his shit will create. But I do want a chance to hold that woman next door in my arms again. I'm getting the feeling that Monica pulled her usual pretend-that-nothing's-wrong-and-it'll-go-away and didn't talk to my dad about the mess he's made here, so my only choice is to face my own shit and do what's right.

My heart pounding with fight-or-fight adrenaline, I pick up the phone. I barely make it through the niceties with his receptionist, so by the time he gets on the line, I'm raring to go.

"Thanks for setting me up to fail, Dad."

There's a slight pause before he answers. "What are you talking about?"

"The feud with your brother? Stealing work from the one woman who does background casting here?"

"The only person doing any stealing is your Uncle Robert."

"Still, you could've given me the entire story before I showed up and stepped right into the middle of it all."

His sigh is that of a man who believes he's the one who's been wronged. "Whatever problem you've got there, I'll wager it's just more of my damn brother twisting the knife. He and his wife are always trying to prove that they're better than we are."

"What happened here, exactly? You told me we were opening the office because you saw potential for growth in the Southeast."

"Apparently my brother saw that too."

"So this *is* about your problem with him."

"Only because he created it," he counters, his smooth tone unwavering. "We cast the pilot for *Lawson's Reach*. When the show went into production a few weeks ago, the line producer said that some girl from the area was doing the local casting. But she was getting paid to do it by your cousin Jay. After I fixed that problem—we had first refusal on local casting, so it only took a quick call between lawyers to get it back —I asked around about her. Several people said she was reliable, so I reached out to her."

"You called Violet?"

"I don't remember her name. What I do remember is that she refused to work with me. So I sent you in. Now you can show her how it's done. While you run her out of business."

Something still smells fishy here, but there are so many moving pieces to this puzzle I'm not sure what to believe. "And what about Uncle Rob and Jay?"

"I just told you. They *thought* they stole the show from me. Wait till they find out that I double-crossed 'em."

Before I can make an argument that it's the locals who will suffer more than his brother, he adds, "Hey, maybe you should try and find that girl."

"Why?"

"Get some dirt on her. If she wants to go up against us, we'll make sure that everyone knows she's a problem. Hard to work with, unreliable, something like that." There's a click on the line. "Got to hop on another call. I believe in you, son."

He's never said those words to me and I can't help but relish them. But the pride quickly fades as I realize I'm back to square one. Before I can finish sorting through it all, the phone rings. Top of my list this morning was to call a temp agency and get a receptionist in here. Now, though, I'm not sure if I want to be here tomorrow. Maybe running is the best solution, after all. Because doing a good job here inevitably means hurting Violet.

The machine picks up the call, but when my sister's voice plays through the speaker, I pick it up.

"Monica, it's me. Listen, I—"

"I'd love to chat about whatever is going on with you, little brother, but I have zero time. We've picked up a movie shooting in Wallington next month, and I've managed to talk the producer into casting a long list of roles locally. There'll be a lot of extras too, so you've got to make nice with your girl there and figure out a way to get this done."

"I just talked to Dad. He wants me to run her out of business."

I can practically hear her eye roll. "Believe me, you do *not* want to mess with extras. They're a total pain in the ass."

"But he—"

"Just don't tell Dad. What he doesn't know won't hurt him."

Crates of background actor info cards line Violet's office. It would be ridiculous to try and reinvent the wheel here. Going behind my dad's back could backfire, but right now it seems like the best first step.

"They'll be in town to scout next week and will want to see some actors," Monica says. "I'll overnight the script. Big names attached to this, and it's all hush-hush for now. Oop, that's my cell phone—gotta go. Good luck."

Before I can take a breath to get a word in, all I've got to talk to is the dial tone. It's likely to be like every post-divorce family gathering—that is, uncomfortable as hell—but it seems I've got to convince Violet to work with me before I try to convince her to sleep with me again.

CHAPTER 7

LAWSON'S REACH, "DISCOVERY"

THE PRESENCE OF A NEWCOMER SOWS FEELINGS OF JEALOUSY.

VIOLET

I'VE NEVER LOOKED FORWARD TO A WEEKEND MORE. I USUALLY end up working through them one way or another. But when the clock clicks over to five this particular Friday evening, all I can think is *thank god I won't have to see Nate again until Monday.*

Each and every moment of each and every day this week I've been tortured by the man. He finally changed his work attire to khakis and golf shirts, and of course he looks better in them than any man has a right to. Our offices have windows that look out onto a central hallway, and when his door creaks open, no matter how hard I try, I can't keep myself from watching his fine behind parade by. I've literally run into him going in and out of the Xerox room multiple times, engaging in an awkward dance back and forth as we attempt to dodge each other. Each time I was thankful my arms were full because it took everything in me to not pull him close and smell him. Or lick him.

Or bite him.

Instead, I'd use my words to bite his head off.

So mature, Violet.

But I'm off now—not that I have actual free time until Sunday. I'm not directing a play at the moment, but I've promised my grandma that I'll help her out at the inn tonight, I've got two acting classes to teach at the Hannah Block Center tomorrow, and I've got a comp ticket to see a musical at Thalian Hall Saturday night, which is a mix of fun and work, since I'm always scouting for new talent and gauging how regulars are developing their skills.

But Sunday is blessedly unscheduled. So when I get a message from Whitney with the news that she's borrowed a boat and everyone in our crew is available Sunday afternoon, my entire body relaxes in anticipation.

Masonboro Island is Wallington's best-kept secret. It's only been a nature preserve for a few years, but we've haunted it since we were kids. No ferry or bridge will get you there; you have to have a private boat to get across the intra-coastal to it. And you have to know where and how to anchor so that your boat doesn't float away or run aground when the tide shifts. Sully got his marine license the minute he turned fourteen, and either he or Whit's parents have always had a boat or access to a boat. When the guys were in California, Dani would occasionally pilot Whitney and me out to the island. But it wasn't the same without all five of us there.

My job for the day is to bring snacks. We'll take a cooler full of beer and soda, and a tent so I can stay out of the sun, and spend the afternoon lounging on the sand, walking the beach looking for sea glass and sharks' teeth, and bobbing in the ocean.

Ford pulls up to the inn right on schedule in the giant car he's had since we were teenagers. Gertie was his first true love, in my opinion. He stored her in his dad's garage instead of driving her all the way across the country. That car being here has always given me hope that he'll eventually return home to stay.

"I am so ready for this, y'all." I climb in the back next to Whit and Skye, who wiggles with joy when she sees me.

"You and me both," Dani says from the front seat as I give the dog all my lovin'. "I swear, I've driven more miles this week that I did all last year."

"How's that going?" Ford asks. "And when did showing writers around become your job?"

"You mean another of her jobs?" Whitney ticks her fingers as she counts. "Location scout, housing coordinator, bartender, and now driver."

"Maybe I can take one of those jobs from you," I grumble.

"Don't you have a brand-new full-time job?" Dani asks.

"*Had* is more like it," I say before zipping a finger across my lips. "But I don't want to talk about that today. I just want to enjoy the company of my friends."

Whitney looks out the window as Ford takes the turn onto Wrightsford Beach Road. "Speaking of which, aren't you going to pick up Sully?"

Ford shakes his head. "He said he'd meet us at the marina." Minutes later, Ford has parked his car, but there's no sign of Sully's truck in the lot.

"Y'all really want to carry all this crap across the island?" Ford asks as we unload. "This tent is huge."

"The tent is nonnegotiable," I say. "You know I'll burn to a crisp without it."

Whitney hooks an arm in mine. "I'm with Vi. I'm trying not to get so much sun this summer. I'm afraid of turning out like my mama."

No one wants to touch that with a ten-foot pole, as everyone knows the woman has spent hefty sums at the plastic surgeon to maintain a youthful look. Only somewhat successfully.

"I quit smoking again too. I found out it's bad for the skin." Whitney shakes her head. "I just hope I don't get fat like last time."

"Oh my god, Whit." Dani swats her with a towel. "You'd be gorgeous if you gained fifty pounds and never made up your face again."

I get why Dani gets frustrated with Whitney. Maybe it's because Whitney and I are onlies, while the rest of the group has multiple siblings, but I have a little more patience with her. So I change the subject. "Which of these vessels is ours for the day? Do we get an ocean liner, a dinghy, or something in between?"

When Ford—who wisely made himself scarce during the discussion of Whitney's looks—returns with one of the carts the marina provides, we load it up. Then Whitney leads us down the walkways to the slip where our borrowed boat awaits. The reflection of the sun on the water is blinding, so I have to squint to make out Sully's form when he greets us from the stern of what looks like a little Carolina skiff. Another male figure is on the bow looking out toward the water. Probably the boat's owner making sure we know what we're doing.

But then he turns around. And my mood goes right off the high dive to plummet into a bucket of despair.

What the fuck is Nate *doing here?*

NATE

When Sully invited me to join him and his friends for an afternoon on Masonboro Island, what he described sounded like a heaven on earth—the polar opposite of a crowded

Malibu or Santa Monica beach. I agreed readily since it's not going to be easy to make friends with anyone on the studio lot. Everyone from the craft services guy to the security guards has made it clear that they are firmly on Team Violet.

Deserved or not, I've been cast as the villain in this picture.

Sully never said who his friends were when he issued the invitation. I assumed it'd be a crew of surfers, part of the loose group of men and women that we've been lining up and dropping in with every morning. So when he calls out a welcome to his friends, the absolute last person I expect to see is the woman who's been driving me insane for the past week. Whether she's throwing eye daggers every time I pass in front of her office windows or cutting me off from the only decent caffeine source on the lot or just making me feel equal parts horny and guilty, Violet haunts my days and nights.

With my luck, this three-hour tour will turn into a *Gilligan's Island* situation with me as the Professor and her as Ginger. That is, her off-limits and out of my league for three seasons and a seemingly endless run of syndication.

Sully seems clueless as he introduces me to his friends, so I guess this wasn't some kind of setup on his part. Poor guy. He has no idea what he's gotten himself into.

Meanwhile, Violet looks even hotter than I could have imagined in a one-piece suit covered by a gauzy wrap that hugs her curves the way I'd like to. In fact, for once I'm wishing for the cold of the Pacific ocean instead of the warmth of the Atlantic, fearful I've got a *Free Willy* situation to deal with. Warm water is not likely to keep my boy caged once Violet reveals what's under that coverup.

I mean, her friends are attractive. They're just not my types, I guess. One's got a Winona Ryder vibe. The other girl reminds me a lot of that blond actress in *I Know What You Did Last Summer*—Sarah Michelle Gellar. Which was shot around here, apparently.

Hopefully, they're not planning to reenact a scene from that movie, that is, murder me and toss me in the ocean.

Deciding to follow Violet's lead on how to play this, I keep my greetings neutral. After exchanging polite greetings with Ford and Violet, Sully introduces me to the other two.

I smile at the women as I help load things onto the boat. "I remember you both from the bar the night I met Violet."

The shorter one, Whitney, tips her head to the side. "You're working in the office next door to her now?"

"I am," I confirm.

"Hm," is her only response.

The motorboat is barely big enough to contain six adult bodies and the dog as well as all the gear. Of course, an ocean liner wouldn't be big enough to contain the unspoken tension between me and Violet, Violet and Sully, and the rest of Violet's friends and me.

At least the dog isn't growling at me. She spends the entire time on the prow, tongue flapping in the wind.

I take a page out of Skye's book and simply enjoy the warmth of the sun on my skin in contrast to the cool breeze created by the boat's swift movement. The views are gorgeous too. Egrets and pelicans and cormorants perch on the ends of docks or fly overhead. Homes dot the grassy shoreline, from shacks tucked into the woods to stately homes with wide manicured lawns leading down to private docks.

We're not the only ones in town taking advantage of the waterway on this cloudless summer day. A veritable parade of other boats of all shapes and sizes power and paddle and sail up and down the waterway. It does seem the best way to escape the heat and humidity.

After a short trip up the intracoastal, Sully steers the boat off the main drag and through winding shallows before easing it toward a little beach. Then everything is hustle and bustle as everyone but me seems to have a role in anchoring the boat and getting everything ashore.

When Sully explains that we'll need to hike several hundred yards across the island to get to the ocean, I load myself up with chairs and a cooler and a bag of towels. A loud sigh from Violet has me catching her eye for the first time since seeing her on the dock. In response, she closes her eyes and shakes her head.

"Is something the matter?" I ask before lowering my voice to add, "I mean, is something *else* the matter?"

She points at my bare feet. "Do you have flip-flops or water shoes?"

Not what I was expecting. "Uh, I have a pair of old sneakers, but I was going to leave them on the boat."

She shakes her head briefly. "The sand on the path over to the ocean side of the island is like molten lava. I even put booties on Skye." She pulls something out of the tote at her feet and calls the dog over. As she covers its paws, she calls to the boat, "Hey, Sully, throw Nate his shoes so he doesn't burn the soles off his feet."

As he does so, Sully gives me a sheepish shrug. "Sorry, forgot to warn you about that."

"Boys," Violet mutters.

"Can't live with 'em, can't kill 'em," Whitney finishes for her, with a smirk in my direction.

At least no one's going to murder me, I guess.

VIOLET

I'm going to kill Sully, and the minute we get to the ocean side of the island I take him aside to tell him so.

"Sully and I are going for a walk," I announce.

Whitney opens her mouth like she's going to ask if she can join us, but after a warning look from me, she changes tack. "I don't know about y'all, but I'm going for a swim."

Once we're out of earshot of the others, I lay into him. "What do you think you're doing inviting the enemy to my one place of escape?"

Sully just blinks at me in that irritatingly Zen way of his. "I have no idea what you're talking about."

His confusion seems genuine, but I'm not letting go that easy. "You didn't know that that man has opened up a casting office next door to mine and is stealing business from me?"

Sully goes hands up. "If by *that man* you mean Nate, I met him at the beach. We've been surfing together. All I know is that he's new in town."

"You didn't think to ask what he's doing here?"

He shrugs. "Didn't come up."

I blow out an exasperated breath. "I'll say it again. He. Is. The. Enemy. And now I have to spend the afternoon with him unless I want to swim back to Wallington."

"Don't you think you're overreacting a little bit, Vi?"

"I am not being dramatic," I hiss, barely keeping myself from stamping a foot in the sand. "I quit teaching to open this business on the promise of a full season of work on *Lawson's Reach*. Then this guy and his big LA casting company come flying in to stomp on not just my dreams but my livelihood."

Sully nods slowly. "I'm sorry that happened to you. But my experience with the guy has been entirely positive. Maybe give him a chance? Or at least try not to poison him or drown him or—"

"Bury him alive in the sand?"

"Or that."

When Sully crouches to pick up a handful of detritus from the sand, I turn away from him to take in the wide expanse of beach, flanked by sea grass–covered dunes on one side and the Atlantic on the other. Unlike Wrightsford Beach, where we'd be lucky to find a space to lay our towels on a sunny July Sunday like this one, there are just a handful of other beachgoers.

"I've missed this place," he says as he sifts through objects in his hands. "And my friends."

It's on the tip of my tongue to point out that while his friends are my friends, the Venn diagram does not include Mr. Hollywood back there, but the whole point of coming here was to remind Ford and Sully of what they've been missing.

"Lookee here," Sully says, holding out his palm.

Two shards of green glass sit side by side.

"I bet both of these started out as a Coke bottle. But this one"—he points to the bright green, sharp-edged one— "would slice your foot wide open, while the other one is a gorgeous piece of sea glass. Which one do you want?"

His words carry no accusation, but I get what he means. My sharp edges could use a little sanding down.

"I'll take both of them. I'll add one to my collection, and I'll put the other in our trash bag."

When he gives me a look that says he's unconvinced that I've let go of my vitriol, I add, "I promise not to use it as a weapon."

After I stow the glass with our things, I grab Sully's hand. "Last one in the water's a rotten egg."

NATE

For a few magical hours, I'm in heaven. I don't know what Sully said to Violet, but she's laid down her sword and let me in. Not to her inner thoughts, but to her inner circle.

I've enjoyed surfing with Sully over the past week, but we haven't hung out other than that. It's interesting to see beyond the unflappable cool he exhibits on the water. I hardly recognize him now, rolling on a towel laughing so hard he's gasping for air at the story Ford's telling about the English teacher that hit on him in high school.

"That's weird," I say. "That's a plot point in *Lawson's Reach*."

Before I can kick myself for bringing up the biggest point of contention between Vi and me, Ford says, "Yeah, that's what happens when your brother's best friend scores a writing gig on a TV show."

This prompts a tear of reminiscences and speculation about which of the friends' seemingly endless escapades will be mined for the teenaged characters' lives.

"Like the girl who climbs in the window to watch movies in the boy's bedroom?" Sully asks.

"Which they turned around," Violet points out without opening her eyes. "Instead, it was Ford who climbed in *my* window."

"I used to row a boat over to Sully's house, just like the girl does in the show," Dani says.

"And I tried out for the cheerleading squad," Whitney adds. "Like in the episode they just wrapped. Remember that? God, I was so awful."

"You were still adorable, honey, don't worry," Dani says.

"Sully was going to try out with me, but he chickened out at the last minute." Whitney's description of Sully's efforts at learning choreography has them all howling with laughter again.

Relaxed in a beach chair under the tent, Violet seems much more like the woman I first met. Since that first night, every time I've caught a glimpse of her through her office windows, she's been angrily punching in phone numbers or pacing back and forth swinging the phone cord or writing furiously on her wall calendar.

I hate that I'm the source of her unhappiness.

Offering her work would be a financial boost, but would it be a bigger blow to her ego? She wanted to be her own boss, so she's unlikely to want to work for someone else again. Especially if that someone is me. Right now, though, the last thing I want to do is remind her of work and all the reasons why she should be mad at me.

We've stuffed ourselves with snacks and sandwiches, and the beer I drank has me slightly buzzed. Several people look like they're about to fall asleep, but I'm not feeling like a nap.

I stretch to standing and grab the Frisbee I brought along. "Anyone want to play?"

The humans groan out responses.

"Ugh, too full."

"Can't move."

"Sorry, no."

But the dog barks. This animal has only ever growled at me. Maybe earning the dog's trust is one way into Violet's good graces. I need all the help I can get if I'm ever going to convince her that I'm not the enemy.

Skye barks again. Tail wagging, ears pricked, and mouth open in a doggy smile, it seems she wants to play.

"All right, let's go, girl."

VIOLET

There's a dog-frisbee competition in Wallington every fall, but while we sometimes throw a ball for Skye, I never thought to play frisbee with her.

Turns out she's a natural.

Nate starts slow, tossing it to her from a few feet away. After just one miss, where the disc bounces off her nose, she figures it out. He seems to know what he's doing, controlling the trajectory so that Skye has to run a bit further each time. Soon she's racing down the beach, leaping into the air, twisting her body to capture the Frisbee with her jaws, then trotting back to drop it at Nate's feet.

Just when I start to worry that she'll overheat, he squats to scratch behind her triangular ears and has a little chat with her before the two of them walk back to the tent.

The smile on Nate's face is triumphant. Not swaggering like he's defeated the enemy. He just looks like he made a friend.

I pour water into a plastic bowl, and Nate takes it from me with a nod of thanks before holding it for her, murmuring, "Good girl. You need that, huh?"

Once she's licked the bowl clean, he flops onto his towel. "Smart dog."

"She is." I give her a kiss on the nose. "She's our girl."

"That's right," Dani adds. "This Carolina dog belongs to all of us."

Nate studies Skye. "Is that a kind of dog or just what you call her?"

"I'm pretty sure Carolina dogs are officially a breed now, but they've been around for hundreds of years in the swamps of South Carolina. A cousin of mine keeps them and this girl was a runt, so he gave her to us." Dani calls Skye over and scratches under her chin. "You're our little dingo, aren't you?"

Nate points at her. "That's what she looks like. I was trying to figure that out."

Dani shrugs. "Lots of wild dogs end up looking like her. Pointy ears, medium-sized, narrow build, bushy tail… something about evolving near, but not necessarily with, humans."

Skye yawns, the rest of us echo her, and a restful silence takes over. I have to admit that Nate has done an admirable job today. It can't be easy, with all of our inside jokes and recycled stories, but he seems okay with being on the outside looking in.

With a yawn, he flops onto his back and stretches his arms

over his head, the muscles of his arms, shoulders and chest flexing and releasing. Just like he did the night we were naked together.

Ford and Sully have muscled chests too, but… This. Man. Just the thought of him hovering over me and caging me in has me restless. Good thing I'm wearing a suit with a built-in bra, or my desire would be clear for everyone to see. It's nowhere near chilly enough for the air alone to have my nipples perking up like they are right now at the sight of him. At the memory of what he's capable of. My sex squeezes with an ache so deep I have to roll onto my belly to feel less exposed.

"Man, this place is amazing," Nate says on a sigh. "I don't think I've ever been on a beach quite like it. And you can get here in under half an hour. You don't have to fly to another country."

"It's insane out here on Fourth of July weekend," Ford says. "But otherwise, it's the quietest beach for miles."

"Wish I could have an office at the beach," Nate says.

His mention of the word "office" shifts my frustration from sexual to emotional.

"Everything down at those studios is so ugly," he continues.

"You'd never get any work done though," Sully says.

"'All work and no play makes Jack a dull boy,'" Nate argues.

"It'd be all play and no work," Ford says with a laugh.

"It's too hard to park at the beach," Whitney says. "Everyone would be late to their auditions."

At *that* word, every bit of relaxation from this idyllic day flies away like a plastic bag blowing down the beach. My hands, needing something to do, begin the process of packing up.

"Like that doesn't happen anyway," Nate says. "I know it's unrealistic, but it would be nice. At the very least, I think I'm going to have to find a place to live near the water."

"Are you planning on staying?" Sully asks.

"I don't really know for sure. Me coming here was kind of a last-minute decision." Nate finally seems to notice the tension that must be radiating off me in waves. "Anyway, I really appreciate the invitation to join you today, Sully. All of you. Thanks for letting me crash your party."

My friends say the right things.

"It was great to meet you."

"Anytime."

"You're always welcome."

I let my silence speak for itself.

CHAPTER 8

LAWSON'S REACH, "DISCOVERY"

LAWSON AND CHARLI GET MORE THAN THEY BARGAINED FOR WHEN THEY SHOOT
A SCENE FOR LAWSON'S MOVIE.

VIOLET

CASTING EXTRAS IS CLOSER TO RUNNING A TEMP AGENCY THAN directing a play. Usually, the job just involves going through my crates of index cards, pulling a group that fit the specs the scene calls for, and then making calls until I have enough people willing to show up at the right time and place.

Sometimes they're provided with costumes, but usually they're asked to bring their own wardrobe. Today the request was for winter gear. I signed in fifty people this morning at 6:30 a.m. when it was already seventy-five degrees. When the thermometer outside my office reads ninety-five, I start to worry. When I get a call from a friend in the production office letting me know that some of the older extras are looking peaked, I drive back to the location to make sure my people are being treated okay.

After I hoof it from the cast and crew lot over to the

outdoor set—sweat pooling between my boobs, my light summer dress plastered to my back—I find my extras standing in the full sun wearing coats and hats and gloves. Just as I'm about to ask a PA why these poor people can't wait in the shade until they're needed, a man steps out of a trailer and takes three steps in the sunlight before ducking under the tent shading Video Village—aka the collection of monitors and tall folding chairs where the producers and director hang out. There's a generator running, meaning this guy has been sitting in air conditioning while everyone else stands around in the heat and humidity waiting for him.

Things move quickly as soon as his butt hits the director's chair, so I don't get a chance to ask anyone to do something to give the extras—quite a few of whom are over seventy years old—some sort of relief. I do sidle over to the sound cart. Without me having to ask, the mixer nods a greeting and hands me a pair of headphones so I can listen in.

The AD calls action, and two top-of-show actors exit the building in heated conversation. The boom man, walking backwards to stay with them, almost knocks over one of the group of extras surging forward. And that's just the first run-through.

After the umpteenth "Cut," instead of the AD calling "Back to one" again, the director gets up so quickly he knocks his fancy-ass chair over. "What do I have to do to get these rednecks to move their fat asses?"

A hush goes over the set. Without thinking, I rip the head-phones off and shove them at the sound guy before hustling as fast as I can to get between this asshole and the crowd of people he has completely disrespected.

"I don't know who raised you," I grit out, "but any woman I know would be ashamed to hear her son speak that way. I need you to apologize right this minute."

The man looks at me like I'm Mork from Ork before

turning to one of the many toadies flanking him. "Who the hell is this?"

I step back into his line of sight. "I am the casting professional responsible for the background actors hired to work on this movie today. Citizens of this town who are proud to represent it by spending a day lending their bodies and voices to your project to make it more realistic. If you can't treat them like the human beings they are, then I am going to dismiss them for the day."

"You can't do that," he says with a sneer.

"Are you going to apologize?"

"If they can't take direction, you can get me another set of extras."

I've been appalled by the rude behavior of movie stars and directors and producers in the past, but this guy takes the cake. Pulling the clipboard which holds the contracts these people signed this morning out of my bag, I remove papers from the clip and slowly tear them all in half. Tossing them at the asshole's feet, I say, "I'm afraid I can't. Get your own damn extras."

He doesn't speak as I stalk over to my people and tell them they can take their coats off and go home, letting them know that I'll pay them for the day. As I walk past him, however, he pitches his voice loud enough that I can overhear what he says to the first AD.

"Isn't there another casting office in town now? Call them and get me fifty extras."

I look over at the AD, who winces when I catch his eye.

"What are you waiting for? Make that call," the director yells, before stalking back to his air-conditioned trailer.

The AD jogs to catch up with me as I walk back to the parking lot. Taking my elbow, he says, "You did the right thing, Vi."

I just nod and climb into my car, biting the insides of my

cheeks to keep from losing it in front of him. Because I just gave Nate everything he needs to shut me down.

NATE

Thanks to a suggestion from Sully, I've got a new receptionist, a retired teacher named Betty Wilson. And not a moment too soon. Things weren't too bad early in the week. Calls were coming in all day, but they were mostly about projects I'm already working on. But today, it's like a spigot got turned on. Not only is the phone ringing constantly, but people are showing up at the door with headshots and résumés asking if I'll be holding an open call soon, if they can schedule a meeting, if there's anything they can audition for.

At the same time, a bunch of men have shown up at Violet's door looking—and one smelling—like they plan to go fishing.

When there's a break in the chaos, I thank my new hire profusely for jumping in and handling things. "I don't know what I'd do without you, Mrs. Wilson."

She waves a hand in the air. "Believe me, anything is easier than teaching eighth-grade math. This is actually fun. And please, call me Betty."

"I just don't get what changed. I promise it wasn't like this yesterday."

Her lips pressed into a flat line, she looks at me sideways. A *don't-bullshit-me* teacher look that sends an involuntary shudder through me.

Even though her unwavering stare makes me feel guilty as hell, I plead innocence. "Seriously, Betty. It has never been this busy."

Finally breaking eye contact, she opens the bottom drawer of her desk and pulls a newspaper from her handbag. She flips it open and points to a large advertisement. "Did you not place this ad?"

"What the fu—um, sorry. I mean, what the heck?"

She pats me on the arm. "Don't worry, young man. I'm done with censoring my mouth. Holding it in for thirty years was enough. You can say all the fucks you like in front of me."

I mumble something in response, but I'm not sure what because I can't believe what I'm seeing. "Carolina Casting" is emblazoned across a quarter-page ad with this office address and the text, "Seeking professional actors as well as local citizens to play extras in television and film productions across the Southeast."

We'd never run an ad like this in LA. I can see the value of an announcement here, where the pool is a lot smaller, but you'd think if he really wanted me to succeed, my dad would've given me a heads-up before doing it.

Then I notice another, smaller ad on the same page. The words "Casting Carolina, now serving anglers in Wallington" are printed above Violet's address.

I pick up the phone to call my father, but another line rings before I can begin dialing, so I hit the flashing button instead. "Carolina Casting, Nate speaking."

"Hello, Nate. I'm the second AD on a film shooting in Wallington. Any chance you could get me fifty extras by the end of the day?"

A week ago, I'd have leapt at the opportunity to prove to my family that I can succeed in this business, but something seems fishy about his request. And it has nothing to do with the stinky gentleman knocking on Violet's door at the moment. "Why the rush?"

"Uh, we had a little misunderstanding with the gal that brought in people today."

"A misunderstanding?"

"Well, between you and me, the director was being a dick,

and she stood up to him. When he wouldn't apologize, she quit. And took the extras with her."

"Was it Violet Davenport?"

"It was," the guy says, sounding pained. "So, what do you say? I'd owe you one."

"I'd love to help you out, but not at Violet's expense. It sounds like your man needs to learn some manners. Good luck with that."

I hang up on the guy with relish. Stepping around the receptionist desk to go back to my office to call my father, I find Violet standing in the doorway, her eyes suspiciously shiny.

Betty greets her before I can recover enough to ask why she's here. "Hello, dear."

Startled, she seems to notice my new assistant for the first time. "Oh. Hello, Mrs. Wilson. Um, what are you—are you working here?"

"Well, I was talking with Joyce Calloway the other day—" the older woman begins.

"Sully's mom?" Violet asks with an accusatory look at me. Maybe she isn't so happy about sharing her friends with me after all.

"Is there another Joyce Calloway in town?" Mrs. Wilson's tone makes it clear that she doesn't appreciate being interrupted.

"No, ma'am, I don't believe there is." Violet answers in a meek voice I couldn't have matched with her moving mouth if I hadn't seen it myself.

"As I was saying," Betty continues, "I was telling Joyce that I was going out of my mind with boredom, and then the next day this young man made me an offer I couldn't refuse."

"What was that?"

"Get out of the house and talk to people."

"Well," Violet says with a polite but dim smile. "Good for you."

"I believe it will be, yes."

"Well, good luck." After that unconvincing seal of approval, Violet turns her full attention my way. "Who were you talking to just now?"

"Some AD looking to replace extras."

"Why did you turn him down?"

"Because whatever happened, I trust that you did the right thing."

"Why?"

"Why would you do the right thing?"

"No, why do you trust me?"

Hands fisted on her hips, the *don't-bullshit-me* look she gives me is eerily like the one Betty flashed at me. Does everyone here think I'm lying all the time?

"A week's observation of how you treat people. And you've never given me a reason not to. Plus, I know how directors can be. Most of them are eighty-five percent fragile ego and ten percent bluster."

"What about the other five percent?" the ex-math teacher asks.

"If you're lucky, talent. If you're not, evil."

"Interesting business," Betty says.

Violet clears her throat. "I'm not sure I deserve... what you said. But I appreciate what you did."

She's almost through the door when I decide to take a chance and ask if she wants the work my sister suggested I throw her way. "Hey, uh, Violet. Hang on a minute."

When she turns back around, her chin's raised in defiance. "Yes?"

"I'm just wondering—I mean, I have some, uh…" My hand flaps uselessly at my sides.

"Spit it out, young man," Betty says.

Betty's words have me straightening up and meeting Violet's flashing eyes. "I don't want to insult your skills—I mean, since you're a theater director, you're probably more suited to auditioning actors than I am. But I do need someone to cover background casting for a few projects, and you're the only one with the contacts. Would you be interested?"

Her gaze tracks to the window and she bites her full lower lip, probably going over the pros and cons.

"If I say yes, I do the job on my terms," she finally says. "You'll pay my rate, and you won't tell me what to do."

"Of course. I would never—"

"Never say never," Betty intones softly from behind me.

"I mean, I assume that—"

"When you assume, you make an ass out of you and me," the teacher voice cuts in again.

I whip around to give her a wide-eyed look that says, *Jesus, let me speak,* which she answers with a pursed mouth, *You know I'm right.*

Clearing my throat, I turn back to Violet. "Of course. It'll be on your terms." Then I remember something. "Except I really hope you won't give extras rides on this show."

Her brows rise in challenge.

"It's just—I think there might be a legal issue—"

She holds up a stop sign hand in front of my face. "Does your father know you're doing this?"

It takes me a moment to shift gears at her change of subject. "Um. No."

"Then I'll do it my way."

Instead of agreeing to that, I blurt out, "Why didn't you just take the work?"

"What do you mean?"

"When my dad called you and offered to contract with you for *Lawson's Reach*. Why didn't you take the work?"

Her expression shifts from defiance to disgust. "Your dad never identified himself. He just offered me business on the condition that I never work with Jay again. Of course, I said no. But I would've if he were the biggest casting director in the world. Jay taught me everything I know, and Fowler

Casting has been my primary source of leads for the past five years. Loyalty is why I said no thank you to your father's so-called offer."

Even though I've watched my father lie to others—including my own mother—even though I know that he'll do anything to get what he wants, it's still a punch to the gut to hear that he'd do it to me.

"What? You don't believe me?" Violet asks.

I shake my head. "Unfortunately, I do believe you."

She hesitates a beat before saying, "All right, then. You can drop by a deal memo and the particulars when you have them, and I'll get right on it."

"Wait," I say before she makes it out the door. "What's your cell phone number in case I need you?"

She exhales deeply, and something tells me it's not one of relaxation. When she turns to me, she looks like my kindergarten teacher did when I'd ask too many questions. "Honey, no one has a cell phone here."

"Beeper?" I counter.

"I have one, but it's only for my grandparents and friends."

"What if there's an emergency?"

"I'm not a doctor. I'm in casting."

"Okay. Well, this is my beeper and my cell."

"I'll take the beeper, but the cell phone number is useless. Coverage here is too spotty."

I'm trying to figure out whether I just made things better or worse when the front door clicks shut and Betty interrupts my thoughts. "I'll just get this computer booted up, and we can write up that deal memo."

"Yes, ma'am," is my only possible response.

VIOLET

I've just finished my first cup of coffee Thursday morning when Sully appears in my office door with Skye at his side. "Mornin'."

"Good morning. Hello, sweet girl." After he unclips her leash, he remains in the doorway with an uncharacteristic frown on his face. "Everything okay, Sully?"

"Everything's fine except that Skye and Mr. Jones do not make good roommates."

We both watch the dog as she goes through her pre-nap routine, alternately pawing at and circling her bed.

"Did she chase Mr. Jones?"

"Did she. All over the damn cabin. Shit went flying, and he ended up crawling under the sink, which connects to the engine compartment. I can't take the boat out until the cat comes out."

"Yikes."

"Mr. Jones was just getting settled on the boat, too. He even went out for a sail the other day."

"Did he like it?"

"I don't think he hated it. He was pretty freaked out at first, but after doing a lot of sniffing the air and watching birds, he settled in under the bimini and took a nap."

"I can take you off the dog rotation," I say. "We just thought it'd be fun to have a timeshare dog, like the way we all took turns with Mr. Jones."

"But Mr. Jones is my cat," Sully says in all seriousness. Like he always does. His nickname through college was actually Mr. Serious. Not that he doesn't have a sense of humor, but it's so dry most people miss it. It's more that he's unflappable. Nothing knocks him off-balance.

Except Whitney.

Thankfully, he seems to have gotten over her. With that

love triangle in our rear window, we can finally all be friends again.

"Riiight. Mr. Jones is your cat. Even though Whit and Dani and I took care of him the first year you were in LA." I hold out my forearm and point to a couple of faint lines. "I have the scars to prove it."

Sully's smile is proud. "He's a tiger, that guy."

Skye huffs from the corner. Hard to tell if she's agreeing or disagreeing. Suddenly, she lifts her head and whines.

"No growl today? Did I win you over with the Frisbee, girl?" Nate asks from the doorway.

Her answer, the little minx? She's on her feet and wiggling her butt at his feet in seconds.

"Hey man," Sully says with a nod. "Where'd you come from?"

Now crouched at the dog's side giving her a butt scratch, Nate looks up. "I work next door."

"Wow, y'all really are rivals," Sully says. "Two casting offices right next to each other?"

Nate's smile dims a bit. "Seems we are the unfortunate victims of a little family feud. My family's feud."

Just as I'm wondering why he used "we" instead of "she" —like, how is Nate a victim here?—my phone rings. "Duty calls."

Sully gives me a salute. "I'll get out of your hair. Sorry about the dog."

I lift a melodramatic hand to my brow. "I'll just have to completely rework the schedule, but I'll survive."

It doesn't look like my act lands, so I reassure him, "It's fine. Now y'all get out of here. Some of us have work to do."

NATE

I really can't blame Violet for keeping up every single line of defense. What my dad did was shitty, and for all she knows, I'm the same. Still, I've put off phoning my father to call him on his crap because…

Well, I'm not sure why.

Why do I crave the man's attention and approval? Just because he's my father? If he were someone else's father, I'd try to gently point out that a narcissist like him is going to have a hard time ever really accepting them for who they are. On some level, I already know it. It's why my instinct is to bail whenever things get uncomfortable.

But I still crave his attention. I just don't act out like I did as a kid. Getting high, fucking up at school, dating so-called inappropriate girls, getting speeding tickets. It all got his attention. But it never lasted.

If he were someone else's boss, I'd counsel them to quit, that whatever they hope to get out of this job, it's not worth it to work for someone who isn't capable of being honest.

Right now, he's my boss *and* my father. Not sure what I'll do if he doesn't admit he was lying—ignore it like my sister does or run away like I usually do—I make myself make the call. Because of Violet.

I have to wait through several minutes of hold music that must be designed to get people to give up and hang up. I'm not sure which is worse canned, the cover of Tom Jones's "It's Not Unusual" or Nirvana's "Smells Like Teen Spirit."

When he finally deigns to take my call, I've had it. "Did you give Violet an ultimatum when you offered her work?"

There's a slight pause before he asks, "Who's Violet?"

Does he really think I buy this act? "The woman who does background casting here in town. And who had planned to do day player casting for *Lawson's Reach*."

"Right. Her. Listen, if she wanted regular work, she

should've taken the deal. More work will come from LA than New York or Boston. So what's the story? Have you shut her down yet?"

"She knows all the actors here. Everyone likes her here."

"So what? I know all the producers and directors, so I've got the contacts to get her the work. Or to make it go away."

"How am I supposed to play catch-up with her? She's got thousands of extras on tap."

"Didn't you see the ad I took out in the paper for you? That'll get you plenty of eager beavers ready to spend a day pretending they're movie stars." I can just picture the sneer on his face. My father thinks extras lie below animals on the performer food chain.

Before I can point out that telling me about the ad would've been a good idea, he asks, "Do you not want to be there? I can send someone else. I've got an assistant here who's hungry to move up."

It takes an act of will I wasn't sure I had in me, but I say, "Nope. I'm here. I'll deal with it."

Better the devil you know than the one you don't, right?

VIOLET

An hour or so later, I've got things under control, including the jobs Nate threw my way. Extras are scheduled for the next two weeks: bar scenes on the indie movie I picked up, a complicated couple days that include boats as well as people on the intracoastal for a big-budget movie that's in town for a few weeks, and people who look like teenagers but aren't for *Lawson's Reach.*

Working with kids is tricky because union rules limit the number of hours they can work. The Screen Actors Guild has less power here than in New York or LA because we're a right to work state. Plus, the union office is up in DC, so it's hard for them to keep track of every little thing going on down here. Out of sight, out of mind sort of thing. A lot of shows will work kids for far longer and far later in the day than they're supposed to, but I try to abide by the rules when I can. In the case of *Lawson's Reach*, where the show uses one of the university buildings for exterior shots, I just called the drama department where I was a major. The secretary put up a notice for me, and the calls rolled in. The college theater majors are happy to skip class for a chance at a bump up to featured extra or a line being thrown to them on the fly during the shoot.

My wall calendars are a mess with all the changes I've been making, and I'd hoped to be doing more than riding herd on background actors this summer, but with the new shows on my schedule, at least I'll make enough to pay rent.

Skye stretches up to standing and ambles over to scratch at the door, letting me know that she needs to do her business. Sully must've taken her on a good run this morning because she's been snoring in the corner since he left. Even so, she can't spend the entire day inside.

As we step out into the hall, Nate is emerging from his office. "Coffee break?"

Skye greets him with a tail wag instead of a growl. "More like a pee break for her."

Nate holds the door for us as we head outside and then falls into step next to us as we circle the parking lot.

"So, what's the deal with the dog?" he asks, watching as she thoroughly sniffs every inch of a tree trunk. "Why do you have her some days and not others?"

"Is she bothering you?"

"Now that she's not growling at me, no."

"She does bark every once in a while. I hope that hasn't messed up any audition takes."

"Nah, I've got that room on the other side from your

office. I just wondered why you only bring her to work every once in a while."

"If you haven't heard her bark, why do you care?" I ask, wondering why he's paying attention to what goes on in my office.

"Just making conversation, Violet. Just trying to be neighborly," he adds in a god-awful attempt at a Southern accent.

"Oh my god. Do not ever do that again."

"Do what?"

"A very insulting fake Southern accent. People will hate you and never forget it. I mean, what if I went to LA and just started in with the 'oh, totally, like, I'm gonna go shopping in the Valley and—'"

"Okay, okay, I get it," he says, hands up in surrender. "But that? Was terrible. Nobody speaks like that."

"Nobody says 'neighborly' like you did either."

"Agree to disagree."

"This is not an agree-to-disagree! I am right."

"All right, all right. You win." He takes a step back, his hands up between us. "And now I am going to beg the craft services man—"

"Randy is his name."

"I am going to go beg Randy for a full cup of coffee."

"He might give you one if you remember his name," I mutter.

Ignoring that, he asks, "Can I bring something back for you? Coffee? Pastry?"

"I'm fine."

"I know you're fine, but would you like coffee?"

"I always want coffee, but I can get it myself, thank you."

"I'm going over there, and I have two hands."

"You think that if you tell Randy you're bringing me coffee, he'll give you snickerdoodles?"

"I'm just trying to be—"

"Don't say it."

"I am extending an olive branch," he says after obviously suppressing both a sigh and an eye roll. "I am truly sorry that you got caught up in the crap between my father and my uncle."

I'm not sure what to say to that, but before I can come up with something, he adds, "Your friends are great, by the way."

"Yes, they are. My friends are the best thing in my life. Besides my grandparents. And this dog. Time to go back to work, girl," I say to her, keeping my voice bright as I push away the tangle of feelings this man has somehow stirred up in me.

"Okay, well, I'll see you," he says as we part ways.

I hesitate by the front door to the production office building, watching him walk away. "Okay!"

He turns around, brows up.

"I would like a cup of coffee. Please."

CHAPTER 9

Lawson's Reach, "Hurricane"

Everyone prepares for the hurricane threatening Harborside.

NATE

It's ridiculous how good it made me feel to get a real smile out of Violet. All it took was the delivery of a cup of coffee and a plate of snickerdoodles. It wasn't the smile she reserves for her dog or her close friends, but it was a wide-mouthed expression of pure joy that would put Julia Roberts to shame.

If I could get a cackle out of her, that'd make my week.

For now, I'm just grateful for baby steps. Plus, I have little time to moon over her because things have ramped up even further at the office.

A big storm's rolling up the coast, so both *Lawson's Reach* and the movie we picked up are scrambling to shoot outdoor locations just in case those locations get erased by the storm. Not something we think about too much in California. I mean, an earthquake could knock a building down at any minute. But here, reports of Tropical Storm Beverly's path are nonstop on the local news and the Weather Channel, so productions have both time and motivation to adjust their schedules. Each adjustment means another round of phone calls to pass on the changes.

Which makes me even more thankful that Violet agreed to take on the background casting. I did offer to take her place getting releases this morning when *Lawson's Reach* decided to shoot local business owners doing storm prep downtown in the driving rain. They don't have a hurricane episode planned, but they want the footage in the can just in case they add one later. But Violet stubbornly refused, saying, "I'm not the Wicked Witch. I'm not going to melt in a damn sprinkle."

Since I don't melt in the rain either, I've made time to surf each morning this week. The storm has meant primo conditions, including big swells and some of the most makeable A-frame barrels I've ever seen.

Still, I wouldn't even try if it weren't for Sully. His knowledge of the area makes it safer to ply the bigger waves, plus he can spot a riptide where I just see a ripple in the water. He's also been incredibly generous with his boards. I have a couple back in LA, but he's got a storage container full of them. Most of which he's gotten second-hand and rehabbed. He shows up every morning with a half a dozen different styles in the back of his truck and has taught me a lot about which boards work best in different conditions.

He called this morning and told me to meet him at the north end of the beach and to park at the spot dubbed the L-Shaped Lot. We were at C Street over the weekend, but between the storm-chaser crowds and the sets the hurricane is serving up, he's decided Shell Island will be our best bet.

When I park next to him just after 6:00 a.m., he's already waxing a Big Wave Gun. I've never used one—I have a Mini-Mal and a short board back home—but I know that the high volume and narrow nose and tail of the Gun will give us both speed and control in the heavy surf. Wordlessly, he points at his board's twin, and I pull it onto the tailgate.

Sully's not a big talker. He's also incredibly humble. The first week we hung out, when I said something about appreciating his laid-back approach to life, he just shook his head and said, "You mean how I'm a directionless fuckup?"

My dad has used those exact words to describe me, but it surprised me to hear Sully say them about himself. "Uh, no," I said in response. "Just because you're not a money-grubbing materialist? That's a positive thing in my book."

At the time he just headed for the water, making it clear that he didn't want to discuss the matter, but I'm pretty sure there's more to the story.

In any case, today I appreciate his quiet presence. It's important to be in a Zen frame of mind when the waves are likely to be challenging. Things can go sideways quickly, so you have to have your head on straight. We smooth the boards in silence until the sky begins to pink up, and then we head for the water.

A handful of people are already out there, and we watch as a huge set cleans a bunch of them up, boards and bodies rolling in what looks like a nine-foot churn.

Sully gives me a look. "You still up for this?"

I take a deep breath before answering. "If they get bigger than that, I might have to bug out, but yeah, let's go for it."

It takes more than the usual effort to duck-dive through the waves. Once we've paddled out past the break, I'm happy to simply take in the shifting kaleidoscope of a sunrise while Sully studies the water.

"The fetch is so long that by the time the waves get here, they're super clean," Sully says.

"Easy to catch," I agree.

"But hell if you wipe out," he says. "Bail earlier rather than later. And remember what I said about the riptide. I don't see one now, but that could change."

After inwardly repeating the mantra to *float, not fight* if I get caught in the trench of water locals call the Rest In Peace Tide because it's so deadly, I give him a nod, and the paddling begins. We alternately speed and slow to find just the right spot to pop up. It takes everything I've got to stay on his tail, but I know he'll guide me on the path of least resistance to the outside.

Once we're up and in the barrel, it's magic. Breathing under the chandelier—lit from above by the dawn light—is like balancing between heaven and earth. By the time we kick out, I'm both exhausted and high on adrenaline.

"You okay?" Sully asks.

"Better than okay." I'm so giddy my words ride a laugh. "Let's do it again."

VIOLET

That damn Tropical Storm Beverly turned into Hurricane Beverly overnight. The weatherman claims she won't hit Wallington directly, but I'm still concerned about my grandparents. They always prepare, just in case, stocking the basement with gallons of water, along with other necessities like flashlights, batteries, a radio, and nonperishables. Not just for themselves, but for any guests that get stuck at the inn.

I just keep picturing them trooping up and down the rickety basement stairs. The last thing either of them needs is a broken hip. So even though I've still got plenty of work to do, I grab my lists and leave the office at two o'clock. After a quick stop at my apartment over the inn's garage to change into clothes I don't mind getting dirty, I head to the kitchen.

"We can't *make* them leave, Mabel," my grandfather is saying as I open the back door.

"I know, Ed," my grandmother says, literally wringing her

hands. "I'm just worried about how we'll feed them if the power goes out."

"We'll make do, like always," he says with a wave of his hand.

The wind blows the door closed, and my grandmother looks up at the sound. "Violet, what are you doing home so early?"

"I just figured I'd rather be here if things get squirrelly."

"Are you hungry? I could make you a sandwich."

"I'm fine, Gran, but thanks." Hands on hips, I take a look around the kitchen. "What can I do to help, Pops? Take things down to the basement? Bring things up? What are we thinking?"

My grandpa shrugs his bony shoulders. "It's a wait-and-see game right now. We're stocked up on everything. Best thing to do is hunker down and hope she blows right on by like they say she will."

Gran answers with an echoing shrug. As always, my grandpa's lean, towering frame makes her seem even shorter and rounder than she is. "If you've got things to do, you go on ahead. We'll call if we need you."

I wag a finger at them. "No hauling things around without me. You've still got a room for Ford, right?" He'd called earlier in the week and asked if he could stay at the inn for a few nights because he'd run out of couches to sleep on. When I get a nod from Gran, I add, "We'll put him to work."

Pops frowns, but he nods his assent.

I have to duck to avoid being hit by flailing tree branches as I pick my way across the yard back to my apartment. Inside, I pour myself an iced tea from the pitcher in my fridge and get to work making calls. The storm has turned production schedules upside down, so I've got plenty of them to make—mostly cancelling extras and putting them on hold until I've got new dates.

By the time I look up from my desk, rain is slashing across

my windows, so I turn on the radio. Out front, water is streaming down the street, but the wind seems steady.

Just as I'm wondering if the forecast has changed, the local NPR anchor breaks into the afternoon classical program. "It seems Hurricane Beverly has a mind of her own, folks. The National Oceanic and Atmospheric Administration is now warning that she'll come ashore just north of Wallington. She's still classified as a Category 1, but stay tuned for the latest."

Throwing on my raincoat and boots, I head back to the inn.

NATE

Tuesday morning, Sully calls to say he won't be surfing because he needs the time to prep his sailboat for the storm, so I skip it as well. Yesterday was a blast, but I've got enough bruises and enough sense to refrain today. Instead, I head to work early. By three o'clock, the lot is looking like a ghost town, so I decide to wrap things up too and head back to the hotel.

As I drive over the bridge to Wrightsford Beach, the wind is whipping up the water of the intracoastal. By the time I pull into the parking lot, it's raining cats and dogs. Pulling my windbreaker over my head and holding my briefcase close, I jog to the entrance. The guy at the front desk just nods, but he looks worried. I turn on the Weather Channel when I get to my room.

The path of the storm they've called Beverly seems to be changing by the minute, so I head down to the bar to grab an early dinner and keep an eye on the news. I've barely finished my food when the bartender brings my check.

"Sorry to rush you, but we're closing. They're evacuating the island."

"Oh, wow. I have to leave the hotel?"

"Uh, yeah," he says, like I'm an idiot. "You can ask about alternatives at the front desk."

There's a long line to do so in the lobby, so I head up to my room to pack an overnight bag. After waiting several long minutes for the elevator, I decide to take the stairs. The lobby is full of people milling about and talking loudly. Just as I'm trying to figure out what to do, I see a familiar face.

Threading through the crowd, I make my way over to him.

"Excuse me, Ford?" I ask.

It obviously takes him a moment to recognize me. "Oh, hey, Nate. Sorry, it's a bit crazy."

"What are you doing here?"

"I used to work here, and the manager called and asked me to help with the evacuation." He blows out a breath as he scans the crowded lobby. "But things got chaotic pretty darn quick."

"I hate to ask, but any ideas of where I could bunk down for the night?"

"It's tough, man. Since Beverly wasn't supposed to come ashore in the Carolinas, none of the tourists left town." He gestures at the front desk, where the clerk seems to be dealing with an irate patron. "All the hotels in town are full, so they're sending people up to Raleigh."

"How far away is that?"

"A couple hours at least."

"Wow. I'd really like to stay in town. I've still got work to do."

"Unfortunately, you can't stay here."

"Okay, well. Thanks for your help."

Before I can turn away, he stops me. "Listen, I'm taking a couple of writers from *Lawson's Reach* to an inn downtown.

You can follow me there, and we can see if they have room for you too. If nothing else, we can share."

"That's so generous of you. Thank you."

"Here's the thing. It's Violet's grandparents' place."

I huff out a laugh. "Well, any port in a storm. Hopefully, they won't turn away a paying customer."

He winces. "Hopefully."

VIOLET

Pops keeps changing the channel back and forth from one local station to the other, but the news is equally bad everywhere. Now that Beverly is headed right at us, it's less safe for people to drive out of town, so the inn remains full. After we manage to feed everyone an impromptu dinner of soup and sandwiches, kids run around downstairs while their parents hover by the television, obsessing over the news with my grandpa.

Dani brought Skye over since Sully and Mr. Jones are staying at her place, but I haven't heard from Ford again. Just when I've started to worry that he's had an accident or something, the front door opens, and he steps inside, soaking wet. Happy to see him safe and sound, I run to grab a towel from the linen closet.

When I return, what I see dims my innkeeper's smile. "Who are your friends, Ford?"

"This is George and Tina. They're writers on *Lawson's Reach*, the ones Dani's been touring locations with. They were at the Rumrunner—"

"And we don't have a car, so Ford offered to drive us off the island," Tina breaks in.

"I knew you had at least one room available, so I brought them here," Ford explains.

Before I can tell him that we have only one room left—the one he reserved—George clears his throat. "I'm sorry, but are you… are you an actress?"

Thrown by the non sequitur, I say, "Not really. I studied it in college, but—"

"I swear I've seen you on TV," he insists before having some sort of epiphany. "Oh my god. You're the stump grinder girl."

I can't help but groan. "Is that thing running already?"

"I think I've seen it twenty times in the past two days," George says.

"Oh, right. I've seen it too." Tina cocks her head to the side. "What *is* stump grinding?"

Shaking my head, I explain, "That was a commercial I shot for a tree service, like, ten years ago. They trot it out every time there's a hurricane because, well, when trees come down, they need—"

"Ever*thang* from trimmin' to grindin', y'all," Ford says, imitating the heavy accent the stupid director made me use for the spot.

When he mimes removing a helmet to shake his hair free just like I did in the commercial, I give him a good swat before turning to our new guests. "If the power goes out, you won't have to see me on TV again."

"Wait, are you stuck now because you drove us, Ford?" Tina asks. "I hope we didn't mess up your plans."

Ford raises a brow, and I give him a *whatever* look. "No problem. I can bunk with Vi."

Tina grins. "It's none of my business, but are you two a couple?"

I can't help but laugh. "Nah, we're friends. We've shared beds since we were kids."

"Weird," George says. "That's in the pilot of the show we're working on. One of the main female characters watches

105

movies in the main male character's house and then sleeps over."

Ford scratches at the five o'clock shadow along his jaw. "Yeah, I saw that in the screening. That damn Sheldon Williams. Anything and everything from our lives is ripe for the picking. But in real life"—he tries to poke me, but I'm too quick for him—"she's more like my sister than my real sister."

"We don't make a habit of sharing a bed anymore," I clarify. Pre-puberty, the lot of us would have sleepovers all the time.

"But when nature gives us little choice…" Ford trails off and shrugs as if that settles the matter.

"Speaking of which, let's get y'all settled before the lights go out," I say.

Ford takes them upstairs, but before I can get back to the kitchen to help Gran, there's a pounding knock at the front door. I hung the No Vacancy sign earlier, but there's always someone hoping for an exception.

When I open the door, that person appears to be Nate.

NATE

Violet ushers me in out of the wind and rain but looks as unhappy to see me as she did a week ago, like the detente we've managed since I refused to poach that job never happened.

"What are you doing here?" she asks, her tone, thankfully, more harried than irritated.

"Uh, did Ford not make it?" I figured he would beat me here. I lost him at some point on the way and had to pull over and study a map to figure out where I was. Even after I got my bearings, I had to repeat the process a couple of times because of downed trees or flooded streets.

"He did. He's getting some people settled upstairs."

"He didn't tell you I was following him?"

"He did not."

"Any chance you've got a room available?"

A host of feelings flits over her features before she schools her expression to neutral. "We don't, I'm afraid."

Not what I wanted to hear, but at least I can sleep on the floor in Ford's room. "Well, in that case, I guess I'm sharing with Ford. He thought that might be the case."

"Unfortunately, he just gave up his reservation to the couple he drove over here."

"Oh." My neurons don't seem to be firing properly, so I'm not quite computing. "Where's Ford sleeping, then?"

She crosses her arms over her chest. "With me. My apartment's over the garage."

"With you?" Jealousy swamps me. "Good for him."

After an impatient huff, she says, "It's not like that. We're friends."

"Right." Hoping that Ford was wrong about the other local hotels being booked, I ask, "Could I possibly use your phone and your Yellow Pages? There's got to be another place with a vacancy."

"Sure." She ushers me to an old-fashioned telephone nook. "Good luck."

VIOLET

Just when I think I've got everything under control—despite the fact that we're over capacity and the man of my dreams and nightmares is dripping rainwater all over the telephone nook while I wrestle with competing ideas for where he should spend the night—the power goes out.

Time to jump into the emergency routine. First up, distribute flashlights. When I bring one to Nate, he's mid-dial.

"Any luck?" I ask.

"None yet," he answers, thanking me for the flashlight.

Conscience pricks me, but before I can offer him the couch —or my bed, with me; hell, Ford can have the couch—Pops calls out, "Violet, we have a tornado warning. We've got to get everyone down to the basement."

Panic has me grabbing Nate by the arm. "I need a favor from you," I whisper.

He stands, filling the tiny alcove. Still, I step closer. My brain has a plan: ask him to escort my grandparents to the basement while seeming to ask for help from them. But my body has other ideas. The look in his eyes tells me he's feeling the same thing I am. Our lips are close enough that I can practically taste the salt on his skin, when I hear my grandpa call, "Violet? Where are you?"

Brain clicking back on, I force my lips toward his ear. "I'm worried about my grandparents navigating the basement stairs. Can you distract them while I get the guests and supplies downstairs so they won't try to help?"

His lips graze my cheek as he nods. "On it."

But before he exits the tiny space, his lips brush over mine, and he whispers, "To be continued."

NATE

I ply Violet's grandparents with question after question about hurricane preparation, their history with storms, and anything else I can think of, while Violet and Ford herd the other guests to the basement. By the time Ford and I get Ed and Mabel safely down the stairs, there are chairs and camping lanterns set up to make the place habitable. Along the way, I learn just how much time she spends taking care of them and the inn.

"We kept it going longer than we'd intended," Mrs. Kennedy explains.

"Because we thought it might be something Violet would want to take over," her husband continues. "But since she's got her own business now…"

"We really should think about selling, but it would have to be the right buyer."

"Someone who's willing to take on an historic building."

After Mr. Kennedy puts his arm around his wife's shoulder, she smiles up at him. "It's not for everyone, true, but we've had so many wonderful experiences over the years."

"We'd want that to happen for someone else."

The way they finish each other's sentences is as charming as the couple themselves. It's been entertaining as well as educational to keep them occupied.

Once everyone is settled, Mr. Kennedy stands and clears his throat.

"We don't want to use up the batteries, so we'll call a curfew in fifteen minutes. I apologize that the accommodations aren't as comfortable as your beds upstairs, but we'll be safe down here. Hopefully, you can get a bit of rest."

After he's back in the lawn chair I fetched for him after we'd negotiated the stairs together, I excuse myself to see if there's anything I can do to help Violet. When I find her, she's answering questions and doling out water bottles. I do get a grateful smile from her, so I take that as a win and find a spot to settle into a folding chair of my own, right next to Skye.

According to Violet and her grandparents, below ground is our best bet, but the wind lashing the building and surrounding trees overhead has me wondering how safe we really are. From the freight-train roars of the storm outside to the creaks and groans of the building itself, the idea of safe shelter seems improbable.

Luckily, I have some distraction in the form of the almost kiss that happened upstairs. Once the lights go out, I let my imagination take me away from it all.

CHAPTER 10

Lawson's Reach, "Hurricane"

While one set of friends and neighbors rides out the storm, Parker and Charli are trapped alone, together.

VIOLET

After a long night of howling wind, where I was kept busy helping people find their way to the closest bathroom as well as keeping an eye on my grandparents, I must have fallen asleep at some point, because the next thing I know, the sun is shining through the windows set high on the basement walls.

I know I'll need to face the mess both outside and inside soon, but I give myself a moment to appreciate the sight across the room from me: Nate asleep. Face relaxed, head tipped back against the wall behind him, long legs stretched out, he looks even younger than he is. Less big-city bad boy, more boy next door. I don't have time to wonder what it'd be like to wake up next to him in an actual bed, however, because guests begin to stir, Skye comes begging to be let out, and I'm back on duty.

Over the next couple of hours, every time I look up from

helping someone, he's doing something for someone else. First, he makes sure my grandparents get up the stairs safely, the same way he skillfully guided them down to the basement the night before—all the while making it seem as if he were just there for a chat. When I go back to the basement to grab a few supplies for a makeshift breakfast, he's folding chairs and tidying up. Later, I find him out in the yard, creating a game out of picking up pinecones with Skye and a bunch of kids.

Perhaps I've judged him too harshly.

I just lumped him in with his family, the people who didn't give a crap that my livelihood would be a casualty of their family feud. I mean, what did I expect? That he'd just pack up and go home in order to save me and my business?

He hasn't done that. Instead, he's stepped up for me. Not just last night, but he's done what he can to help me out within the confines of an ugly situation that I'm pretty sure he had no part in creating. I'm thinking that it's time to bury the hatchet between us when Dani pulls up in front of the inn.

I give her a hug, and we trade reports on damage from the storm. Turns out we were both lucky. Neither her house nor the inn suffered terribly, though she says that tornados must've hit a few areas of town, from what she saw on the drive over.

"But that's not why I'm here," she says, her brow creasing. "I'm worried about Ford and Whitney and Sully."

"What do you mean?"

"This morning, after Ford left your place with George and Tina, he stopped by to check on us. When he found out that Whitney and Sully spent the night together at the KMart—" She breaks off and shakes her head. "The look on his face? He could've chewed up nails and spit out a barbed wire fence."

"Whoa, back up." I wave a hand in the air between us. "Whit and Sully spent the night at the KMart? Why?"

Arms crossed in front of her chest, she groans. "They ran

over there last minute to pick up some supplies. Just when I was starting to worry about them, thinking they shouldn't be out driving with the tornado warning, Sully calls from a payphone inside the store. They got locked in somehow, and nobody—from the police to the store manager—was willing to go out in the storm to unlock the doors."

"That's crazy. And you think Ford is jealous?"

"Whitney's been dating people, but neither Sully nor Ford ever talks about girls back in LA or here. Maybe neither of them has really gotten over her."

"So where are they now?"

"Driving to Raleigh. Whitney called from a filling station halfway there, all giggly—you know how she gets."

"But Ford was driving those writers to Raleigh."

"And Ben Porter too. He got stuck here last night and wanted to fly back to Boston."

"That's a full car, even for Gertie."

"Oh, and Ben's dog."

"I'm still confused. You're worried because…?"

"I just think somethin's gonna blow when they get up there. I think Whitney's playing with fire."

"It can't be all her fault. She's told them time and again that she is not interested in either of them like that."

"There's what you say and what you do," Dani says with a frown.

"Come on. Whit flirts with everybody."

"Well, I guess we have to hope that nobody loses their head when they're all three together. Without us to run interference."

"Sully and Ford have spent the last few years working side by side. They have to have worked it out by now."

"You'd think." She sighs and looks around the yard which, thanks to Nate and the kids, is almost clear of debris. "Well, I just wanted you to know. I've got to go back and finish cleaning up."

"Do you have power?" I ask as I follow her over to her car.

"Not when I left." She opens the door on the driver's side. "Didn't look like it was on anywhere on the drive over, either."

"I hope it comes back soon. We've still got guests staying."

"All right, girl. Come over and let me know if you hear anything."

"Same to you," I call. I hope that she's wrong about the tension between our friends. Meanwhile, I'm going to try and do a little peacemaking of my own.

NATE

After several hours of yard cleanup, I'm a sweaty mess. Since I don't have a room here, I don't have access to a guest bathroom. I did notice an outdoor shower by the garage, which would serve to at least rinse off the dirt sticking to my skin.

I find Violet and her grandmother in the inn's large kitchen, assembling a tray of afternoon snacks for the guests who have elected to stay, despite the lack of electricity. Violet does so much here, on top of her work at the casting office. The close relationship she has with her grandparents makes me wonder if her parents are even alive.

"Did you need something, dear?" Mrs. Kennedy asks.

"Oh, I was just wondering if I could use the outdoor shower." I pull my T-shirt away from my torso. "I got a bit messy out there."

"You really didn't have to do all that work," the older woman says, picking up a bottle of water and bringing it to me.

I demur, thanking her for the water. It was useful to work off a bit of sexual frustration with physical exertion. Not that I can explain that to the pink-cheeked, white-haired woman smiling up at me.

"Violet," she says. "Can you get this young man a towel and show him how the lock works?"

"Yes, ma'am," Violet answers. Her tone is all innocence, but there's something to the glint in her eye that has me raring to go enough that I shift my duffle bag to hide the evidence.

"I appreciate it," I say as I back out of the room and follow Violet down a hall, where she pauses to grab a couple of towels before heading out the back door.

"There's a lock on this shower?" I ask as I follow her down the path, mesmerized by the swing of her hips.

"My grandparents put in the shower back when I was a teenager. My friends and I would use it after a day at the beach so we wouldn't bring sand inside. The lock is mainly to keep the critters out, but it also provides a bit of privacy."

Her voice is businesslike, but the look she shoots over her shoulder smolders, so it's hard to read her intentions. Still, I'm optimistic. The heat between us last night was not just about the lack of air conditioning, and I caught her watching me with an appreciative smile multiple times over the course of the day. I may have pulled off my shirt at one point just to up the stakes. Since she quickly turned away and fanned herself with the empty tray she was carrying, I think I may have scored.

As she stretches to reach through a neatly cut circle in the wooden door of the shower, her short sundress slides up, revealing an expanse of tantalizingly creamy thigh.

"You mind showing me that again?" I step closer to murmur into her hair. "I got a bit distracted there."

She turns to face me. "Distracted? By what?"

She can flutter her eyelashes in faux confusion all she wants, but her pupils, wide with lust, tell me the real story.

"You'd call for a retake if you saw that kind of bullshit on camera," I say with a grin.

"I don't know what you mean," she says, her heaving chest belying her guileless tone.

Stepping closer, I trail a finger from her waist to just under her breast. When she turns into my touch, I keep going, stopping to caress a rock-hard nipple. Her answering moan has my other hand sliding behind her neck, my fingers tangling in the curls that have escaped from her messy bun. Her eyes flutter closed, but her lips find mine without guidance. Needy little sounds puff out as my tongue dips into her mouth for a taste. I press her into the door, needing to feel more of her, but instead of flattening against it, she yelps and stumbles backward.

One arm snags her by the waist, the other catches the doorframe, and I manage to keep us from falling. Just. She laughs as she scrambles to find her balance, but she steps out of my embrace to do so, which has me growling with impatience.

"Down boy," she teases. "I did bring an extra towel."

She closes the door behind me, hooking a rusty latch to lock the door. "The kitchen isn't far and the windows are open, so we'll have to be quiet."

She pulls her dress over her head in a whoosh, and I'm treated to the sight of lush curves adorned by strips of cotton and lace. Then those are dispensed with too. As she reaches into the shower itself, she gives me a quick once-over. "You gonna take those off or what?"

Scrambling to comply, it's not until I follow her into the stream of water that it registers. There's no hot water. "Yikes!"

"Shhh!" she hisses.

"I don't think anyone's going to mistake that for anything other than what it was. Utter shock," I say over chattering teeth. Looking down at my shrunken junk, I add, "And nothing's happening with this guy anytime soon."

She just grabs a bar of soap from a little shelf and begins to lather up. "We'll just get clean and then go upstairs to my apartment. To get dirty again."

Desire warms my blood as I watch her run soapy hands over her own body. "We'll have to try this again when the power's back," I say, forcing myself under the cold stream.

Once we're both wrapped in towels, we grab our clothes and sneak up the back steps to her place. Inside, she leads me to a bedroom. It's stuffy and hot, and I'm already wishing for the chill of the shower again, but when she drops the towel and flops onto the bed, all I can do is follow.

I've never met a woman so confident in bed, so clear about what she wants and when she wants it. My lips and hands are happy to do as she commands.

Until she's slick with desire and my guy's ready to go and suit up. Then I take charge and roll her to her belly. After I pull her hips into mine, she reaches through her legs to position me just so. I ease inside, intending to take things slow, but she has other ideas. Her round bottom rolls tantalizingly, and she draws my hand to her cleft. Brushing curls aside, my fingertips circle and press until her inner walls shudder. As I stroke in and out, they hang on like they'll never let go.

"Jesus, woman," I say on a half-laugh. "You're strong."

She just orders me to keep moving, so I obey, one hand keeping me upright, the other continuing to tease until I'm rewarded with a keening that has me teetering on the edge. All I can do is hang on for the ride. She takes my thrusts with a tightened core that sucks me in deeper and deeper until the moment she lets go, and that has me following her into oblivion.

VIOLET

"Wow" is the only word I can find after Nate collapses onto the bed next to me.

He laughs and slaps me on the bum. "You are a she-devil."

I turn my head and swipe hair out of my face to give him a side eye.

"In all the best ways," he assures me.

"So much for being quiet," I say with a wince.

"So much for washing off the sweat," he adds, a finger trailing down my damp spine.

"I never thought I'd be happy that my grandparents are losing their hearing…"

"And I never thought I'd be happy for a natural disaster."

"Sometimes Mother Nature has to take matters into her own hands, I guess."

"It's not nice to fool Mother Nature," he says, imitating the voiceover from the old margarine commercial.

"I'll keep that in mind." Unfortunately, it isn't long before the post-sex hormone high is replaced by a niggling worry. I may have forgiven him for his transgressions at the office but we just jumped into the sack again without discussing other realities. "So, uh, we never got around to this before, but—you're not seeing anyone back in LA, are you?"

"I'm not, no," he assures me. "And monogamy is important to me."

"Me too. As well as being upfront about expecta—"

Suddenly, the fan over my bed turns on, interrupting me. "Wow. Power's back. That was fast."

He goes spread-eagle on the bed. "Ahh, that feels so good."

Lust shoves worry aside but is quickly overmastered by responsibility. The gorgeous manhood laid out before me is so

118

tempting. But if I don't get back, I know my grandparents will overdo it.

So I get dressed.

"What are you doing?" he asks over a yawn.

"Duty calls. I've got to go help my grandparents, or they'll be doing all kinds of manual labor themselves. I'm not sure how long I'll be." At his groan, I give him a pat on the shoulder. "Feel free to stay and nap if you want."

He pauses mid-stretch to sit up, slapping his hands on his thighs. "You think I'm going to laze around while you dig ditches and haul rocks? I may be a jerk, but I'm not that big of a jerk."

The tiniest bit of an edge riding his words draws me back to the bed. "I was just thinking you might need to rest up for round two."

He grabs me and pulls me on top of him so that I can feel exactly how little time he needed to recharge.

"Woman, with this luscious bod on my rod, I can be ready to go anytime."

I lean down to give him a quick kiss, which turns into a longer kiss, which turns into me plastered on top of him.

But then he breaks it. "All right, all right, I guess I'd better earn my keep here."

This time it's me that says, "'All work and no play…'"

"How about we try 'business before pleasure'?"

"I can get on board with that. One. More. Last. Final. Kiss," I say, punctuating each word with a kiss down his toned chest. "And then we'll table this for later."

He rolls off the bed and jogs to the bathroom to dispose of the condom before getting dressed. When he reappears, he asks, "So, if the power's still off at the Rumrunner, does that mean I'm invited back tonight?"

"You haul enough rocks, you'll get a free shower, too."

He bows formally, gesturing for me to precede him. "I'm all yours."

The words echo in my ears as we troop down the stairs. Words I couldn't imagine him saying a week ago.

Of course, before that, I'd had no idea he'd be my biggest rival.

Wonder what the next episode will bring.

CHAPTER 11

Lawson's Reach, "Detention"

The truth comes out, but it's not what Lawson and Parker were hoping to hear.

VIOLET

Once the power's back on, the hurricane holiday is over and the next day is back-to-back phone calls as each and every production company I'm working with scrambles to reschedule in Beverly's wake. When I stop in to pick up messages from Mrs. Wilson, I notice a printed calendar on her desk. When I ask where it came from, she explains that Nate creates them with some computer program.

I'm not sure I'm ready to let go of my giant wall calendar, but the color-coding on that computer printout was super cool. One way or another, I'll have to replace the dry erase boards soon. I've had to erase and rewrite schedules so much lately, the thing is getting smeary.

A couple of the shows have shifted everything indoors to the stages while they wait for exteriors to get cleaned up, which means they need fewer background actors. Meanwhile,

Lawson's Reach is actually filming the damage for a storm episode now in the works and has requested a handful of extras for that. Seems a bit ghoulish to me, but I keep opinions to myself.

In the few moments when the ringing of the phone goes quiet, I find myself replaying the extracurricular activities of the day before, which winds me up with equal amounts of desire and worry. I may have spent the last week hating Nate, but that didn't stop my body from missing the connection we found the night we met. Still, here at work, I'm not quite ready to trust that he's got my best interests at heart. I don't even know how long he'll be in town. At the same time, I'm not willing to shut it down and miss out on more of the best sex I've ever had.

I'm deep into reliving one of the better moments from yesterday that *didn't* involve sex—Nate's yowl in the shower as the cold water hit—when I realize the phone is ringing. When I answer, it isn't yet another AD or production assistant on the phone, it's Dani.

"Hey, Dan. I'd love to chat, but I'm a little busy here."

"Just wanted to give you a heads-up. I called Ford's brother's house this morning to make sure they knew that the power is on in most of the county."

"Okay…?" I prompt when she doesn't continue. "I don't want to be rude, but my other line's likely to light up any minute."

"Well, the long and the short of it is, Whitney somehow found a rental car and drove back by herself last night."

"Why? Did she have to work?"

"She did, but apparently she also 'didn't want to spend another minute with the two of them.' That's a direct quote."

I can't help the sigh of impatience that escapes my lips. "So? They're grown-ups. It's long past time for them to figure this shit out."

"Do you *want* Ford to go back to LA?"

"I don't think we have to worry about that," I reassure her. "He's looking for work here in town."

"I think we might have to hold some sort of peace summit. To make sure."

"It took thirty years to get to the Good Friday Agreement and end the Troubles in Northern Ireland this spring," I remind her.

"Maybe we can call President Clinton in. He got that Dayton agreement put together much faster."

"Yeah, because he's not so busy right now dealing with his own troubles." When she doesn't come back with a comment about Monica Lewinsky, I ask, "Seriously, Dani, what is it you want to do?"

"Cookout at my house. Tonight. Before things get too out of hand."

"Can I bring Nate?" After several beats without an answer I ask, "You still there?"

"Sorry. I thought you just asked if you could bring your mortal enemy."

"We had a bit of a reconciliation during Beverly," I say, keeping my tone as cool as possible. "It's not him I need to hate, it's his dad."

"Was that orgasms or evidence that got you to this conclusion?"

"No comment. But I do think having him there might keep people polite."

"I'm not sure that's what we need, but if you think it'll help to have a neutral party on hand, then fine."

"What about you and me? Aren't we neutral parties?"

"I don't know about you, but I for one have plenty of opinions about how they got into this situation."

I'm pretty sure Dani blames Whitney for this mess. I don't think it's all on her, but I'd hate to have one or both of my friends disappear for another seven years.

"I guess we have to do something. I'll see you tonight."

NATE

On my way to fetch coffee, a peek in Violet's window makes it clear that she's swamped, so I pick up a cup for her too. When I slip inside her office to place the steaming cup and a seven-layer bar on her desk, her smile is all the thanks I need. Planning to sneak back out again, I wave a goodbye, but she raises a finger and mouths, "Wait a sec?"

I nod and lean on the door while she finishes the call, enjoying the view. Wishing I could enjoy the view all day long. Wondering if we could somehow figure out a way to work together as well as spend every night together.

And then I remember that our what-are-we-doing-here conversation was cut off yesterday by the whir of the over-head fan. Just when I'd been about to say something really sappy like, *I think I've finally found not just a place where I'd like to settle, but a woman I'd like to settle with.*

Thing is, I have no idea what she wants. We didn't pick up the conversation last night because we both collapsed into a deep sleep after another shower and another hot-as-hell roll in the hay. Then, since we slept late, there was no time to talk before work this morning.

Before I can stew further, she hangs up and dives for the cup of coffee. After taking a sip, she sighs with bliss. "I can't even tell you how much I needed that."

"Glad to be of service."

"Would you like to continue to be of service?"

My imagination goes immediately to all the ways I could do so, but with the office windows and Mrs. Wilson on the other side of the paper-thin wall, it'd turn into the kind of movie that neither of us works on.

"Not that kind of service," she says, apparently reading

my mind. "In a different setting, of course, I'd love a repeat of yesterday's adventures."

"I'm sure that can be arranged."

"But my phone's crazier than usual, so I'm just going to cut to the chase. There's some awkwardness between Ford and Sully and Whitney that needs some smoothing over. Dani's having everyone over tonight to try and negotiate some sort of detente."

"Uhh… and since you and I have done such a good job of working things out, you want my help?"

She laughs, not bitterly but not with real humor either. "I'm not sure we're quite there yet. You're still taking work from me. I just think that having you there might keep the boys from doing something stupid."

"Like what? And what's the awkwardness about?"

Her phone rings. "You know what? Don't worry about it. Dumb idea."

Before she can pick up, I place a hand over the receiver. "I want to help. How about I drive you there and you can fill me in on the way?"

She hesitates for a moment. I can't quite read what's going on behind her bright green eyes, but after another insistent ring from the phone, she says. "Sounds like a plan."

I remove my hand, give her a little salute, and walk myself and my coffee next door. The fact that she's asked for my help feels like a win, and I'll take that for now.

VIOLET

I never leave the office right at five, but if I were to wait for the phone to stop ringing, I wouldn't leave at all. Plus, worry over what's happening with my friends and the desire to feel Nate's lips on mine again are enough for me to get my butt out of the chair and turn on the answering machine for the night.

When I walk into his office next door, Mrs. Wilson is gone, but Nate is still on the phone. "You know, I think that'll work."

He writes an address on a notepad and asks a few more questions before hanging up.

"Mrs. Wilson cut out early?"

"Yeah, she had a softball game."

"I have to admit that I'm still a little afraid of the woman."

Nate laughs. "Betty? She's a sweetheart."

"Not how I'd describe her. But to be fair, it could be that I just lump her together with the whole junior high experience." An involuntary shudder goes through me. "See? I get the heebie-jeebies just thinking about it."

Nate nods sagely. "Say no more. Back to the present day where I am, thankfully, no longer sporting a mullet, I have a question."

"Shoot," I manage over a giggle as we cross the parking lot.

"No pressure," he begins. "But if you want to leave your car here overnight, I'd be happy to give you a ride to work tomorrow."

"After you spend the night?"

"Well, I didn't want to assume, but I would say yes to such an invitation," he says with an unconvincing air of nonchalance.

"I could be talked into issuing such an invitation."

"What would it take?"

"Maybe a little reminder of what I'd be missing?"

After scanning the parking lot to make sure no one's watching, his arms encircle my waist. Even though it's still sticky hot out, my skin seeks his. The brief touch sends a quake of desire through me.

He leans back. "That wasn't another shudder of dread, was it?"

"Oh no, that was a shiver. Completely different response."

"Good. I look forward to stirring up more of those."

The man hasn't even kissed me, and I'm all aquiver with lust. I take a step back. "Okay, I guess we'd better get this show on the road before it gets derailed completely. To mix a couple metaphors."

"Am I driving?"

"You bet your sweet bippy you are." He opens the passenger-side door for me, but I wince at the heat radiating from the car's interior. "As long as the AC works on this rental car of yours."

"I'll crank it up high," he promises.

I flap my skirt up and down while the car cools down. Until I realize it's distracting Nate, that is. Pointing at the windshield I order, "Keep your eyes on the road, mister."

After giving him directions to Dani's, I follow up with the *Reader's Digest* version of the love triangle story. "The five of us have been friends since we attended a hippy-dippy kindergarten together. We were from very different backgrounds, but the school was so small that we were the only ones in our class. We stuck together once we got to first grade at the public school. Everything was hunky-dory until Whitney got boobs in tenth grade. Then, a bunch of things happened. Her parents got all weird about her spending so much time with the boys, Ford got all moony over her but wouldn't admit that he liked her that way, even though it was obvious, and everything just got awkward for a while."

"I never had girls as friends," Nate says. "Even my sister's friends treated me more as a mascot, if I was lucky. More often I was just an annoyance."

"Trust me, we were all pretty annoying for a couple years. Especially Ford. And Whitney too, kind of. She started doing that thing a lot of girls do where she's only ever in flirt mode around men.

"But then we got to college, and we banded together again. Doing plays and making little movies. And everything was good until graduation—the party afterwards, to be more specific."

As I picture the ugly expressions on Sully and Ford's faces that night, my stomach turns. Maybe it wasn't such a bright idea to bring Nate along for this.

"What happened?"

"Sully and Whitney got drunk. Well, we were all a bit drunk. But Sully and Whit kissed, Ford walked in on them, and there was a lot of yelling and screaming. Ford had wanted to kiss Whitney for, like, forever but had never made a move. Things were tense after that night, but nobody talked about it. We had all signed on to work together for the summer—at the Rumrunner, actually. I thought they'd gotten over it because Whitney was very publicly dating lots of other guys and Ford and Sully seemed okay. But then one night it came up again, there was another fight, and then suddenly, Ford and Sully moved to California together."

"Wow."

"Yeah, wow. We've barely seen them since. But then the guys got a movie that shot here this past spring. That wrapped a month ago, but they've both stayed in town and have been talking about sticking around. It seemed like they were over Whitney. But something happened the night of the hurricane, and now we have to deal with it again."

"And I'm coming because…?"

"I thought maybe you'd be a moderating presence. But if you don't want to be there, I totally understand. You already had to deal with me being a bitch when Sully brought you to Masonboro."

"Do you want me there?"

"Maybe?"

"Then I'll stay. Unless someone asks me to leave."

He bites his lip, the plump lower lip that is somehow plush and firm at the same time. I'm just about to suggest that we take a detour over to my apartment before going to Dani's when he says, "I hope it's not going to be a problem, but I just told Whitney's mother that I'd sign a short-term lease on a place they own downtown."

This is not where my mind was going, obviously. "Huh? How do you know Mrs. Moore?"

"I ran into Whitney at the catering truck last week and got to talking about local real estate. I was looking for a rental close to the water, but after going through that hurricane, an apartment downtown seems like the wiser choice. On top of that, they've found structural damage at the Rumrunner and are closing to do repairs, which means I don't have time to be picky. Mrs. Moore is letting me take the place month-to-month, so other than the fact that it doesn't have an outdoor shower, it's perfect," he adds with a sexy faux pout.

"Well, you'll just have to borrow mine after you go surfing. And I can ogle you from above."

"Or join me down below."

That image has my brain taking off with yet another round of fantasies, but the reality of what he said catches up with me. He's planning on staying. At least for a bit.

Eyes on the road, he asks, "Sorry, do I go left or right here?"

I have to take a moment to figure out where we are before giving him directions. Then I circle back. "You never really said how long you were planning to stay."

"I'm not actually sure. I just promised my dad three months."

Before I can process that information, we've arrived. Neither Ford's nor Sully's vehicles are here, but Dani and Whitney are visible through the large picture window. Unfortunately, it looks like they're already getting into it.

"You sure you're up for this?" I ask.

"If I ran every time my dad yelled, I'd be on the other side of the planet." He holds out his hand palm up. When I lay mine on top of it, he gives me a squeeze that is somehow both reassuring and a reminder of other things he could be doing with that hand. "If they kick me out, I'll go. Otherwise, I'm here."

"Thanks, Nate. You're nicer to me than you need to be."

By the time I make it inside, Dani is yelling, something she never does, and Whit is crying, something she does too often. Poor Skye is in the corner, ears back and eyes tracking back and forth between them.

When we step inside, only the dog seems to notice our presence. She slinks over to press her body against Nate's legs.

"You're torturing them," Dani shouts at Whitney. "Neither will give up if they think they have a chance with you."

Whitney shakes her hands as she paces back and forth. "I just wish they'd get over it. Over *me*."

"Do you love either of them?" I ask, pitching my voice high enough to get their attention.

Both women turn to face us, but only Dani seems to take in Nate's presence.

"Yes, I love both of them," Whitney cries, practically stamping her foot with impatience. "I love you and Dani too. I need all of you like you wouldn't—I mean, I—"

She seems to be spinning out, so I speak slowly and softly. "Do you love them romantically?"

She collapses on the couch and rakes her hands through her hair, mussing it. Something she never does. "I don't know. I'm so confused. At first, I thought things were better when they came back this time, but it's actually worse. They watch me like hawks, counting every little smile or touch as a win. It's like there's some scorecard that only they can see."

"But what do *you* want?" Dani asks.

"I don't know," Whitney moans, rocking her head on the back of the couch. "To not be the problem anymore."

"Can you just tell them once and for all that you don't want to be with either of them?" I ask.

"I tried that after graduation, remember? And then they ran away together." We all sit with that truth for a moment before she whispers, "I just want everyone to be happy."

"Does that include you?" Dani asks, like she really wants to know.

Whitney's answer is a resigned shrug followed by a tiny shake of her head.

"And that's why everyone loves you," Dani mutters.

NATE

When Sully walks in Dani's front door, I barely recognize him. And it's not just that his beard is gone, although he looks about ten years younger without it. Every time I've been out on the water with him, he's all about going with the flow, like that's his purpose in life as well as the best way to catch a wave.

Now, as he stands in the archway leading into the living room, his jaw is set and his eyes dart around the room like he's searching for something. Or someone. When they find Whitney, his arms cross over his chest. But when Ford opens the front door behind him, his arms drop, his hands fist, and he walks to the other side of the room without acknowledging the guy I thought was his best friend.

I'm not sure why Vi thought bringing me to this show-down at the OK Corral was a good idea. When Sully finally notices that I'm here, he just frowns in confusion. It's clear that my presence is not welcome.

Before I can excuse myself, Violet gets up from the couch

to pull me aside. When she mouths, "Please stay," I don't argue. Instead, I do my best to melt into the background, just like I did as a kid every time my parents fought.

Violet clears her throat. "Look, guys. I don't know what's going on, but maybe we should clear the air so nobody jumps to conclusions and does something stupid."

"Seems like someone already did something stupid," Ford spits out.

Sully spins to face him. "You want to say something to me, just say it."

Whitney jumps up from the couch. "If this is about me, I think I get to speak first."

"Of course it's about you," Dani yells. "It's always about you!"

"Okay, okay," Violet says, spreading her hands wide. "Let's just take a big breath and think before we speak."

"What were you thinking when you went out in the middle of a hurricane?" Ford says to Whitney, his jaw so tight the muscles bulge. "You could've been killed driving around like that."

"She hadn't hit when we left," Whitney says, her chin lifted in defiance. "And the weather report was still saying that she'd stay offshore."

"I know Dani had plenty of supplies," Ford says. "She's always prepared. So what was it you needed so badly?"

A look passes between Sully and Whitney. His nostrils flare, and her eyes go wide.

Ford points at Sully. "I knew it. You're hiding something."

"Oh, for god's sake!" Whitney cries. "I wanted cigarettes. Okay? I was upset and I wanted a smoke and Sully said he'd drive me."

"I thought you quit again," Violet says.

"You can never really quit. At least I can't. Anyway"— Whitney spins to face Ford again—"getting stuck there was all my fault. We went out because of me, and we got stuck at the KMart because I had to pee and the lock was broken on the bathroom door and I made Sully keep watch. By the time I was done, they'd closed the store early and locked us inside."

Ford ticks a narrowed gaze back and forth between Sully and Whitney. "Something happened, though. I mean, you shaved his damn beard."

"Because it was horrible!" Whitney says. "I'm a beautician. I've hated that thing since he grew it two years ago. We played Battleship and I won, and my prize was to get rid of the beard."

Ford doesn't look like he's buying it. "And where did you sleep?"

Sully takes a step toward him, vibrating with outrage. "When's this going to end, Ford? When are you going to let her go? Isn't it obvious that she doesn't want to be with you?"

Whitney whirls on him. "Don't you put words in my mouth!"

Sully's hands open out, palms wide. "I'm just calling it like I see it."

"Sakes alive!" Dani gets on her feet too. "Why do you all get dumber than a bag of hammers when sex is on the table?"

"Just because you've never been in love—" Ford begins.

"Don't give me that 'in love' bullshit." Dani jabs a finger from the guys to Whitney. "If y'all really cared about each other, you wouldn't fight. End of story."

"Not everyone is your mother, Dani," Violet says quietly.

Dani wheels on her. "Y'all are sure acting like her, and all my aunts and cousins too. And yes, I'm talking about you too, Vi. Dicks and vaginas, that's who's in charge in this room."

Violet's mouth gapes, so I clear my throat. "Maybe we should, uh, try to calm down a little bit."

"You don't know what the fuck you're talking about," Ford snaps at me. "Why are you even here?"

"Because I asked him to be," Violet says.

"I thought you hated the guy," Sully says.

"I did." Violet's fists land on her hips. "But we talked through things and realized that we don't have to be enemies. Like maybe y'all could do here."

"I think this is a little more complicated," Ford scoffs.

"Really?" Violet says, her voice rising. "You think losing everything I've been working on for the past five years is no big deal?"

"Jesus. Just stop!" Sully roars. "This right here is quite simple. Whit just needs to make a choice once and for all. And I'll make it easy. I'm taking my boat and going out for a few months. I was going to wait until the fall, but I'm done with this drama."

He steps closer to Whitney and takes both her hands. "I'd like you to come with me. We could figure out if there's something between us. Away from it all."

When Whitney's eyes dart toward her friends, Sully tugs on her hands. "It's not about them. You need to decide based on you and me."

She squeezes her eyes shut and presses her lips together, but her breath hitches and tears leak out anyway. No one moves for I don't know how long, but at some point, her hands slip out of Sully's and she steps back. "I can't."

Sully's nostrils flare once, but then he nods and turns away.

Ford whispers, "Whit?"

But she just shakes her head slowly. "I. Can't."

Ford nods his head just as slowly. "I guess that's it, then."

"That's it? What's it?" Violet asks.

"So, everything's clear?" Dani asks. "We can move on now?"

Ford releases a huff of derision. "Yeah. I'll be moving on. I'm going back to California."

"What? Why?" Whitney asks.

"If you don't know the answer to that, then all the more reason why I need to go."

"But we're friends. Friends stick together," Violet pleads.

"Enough with the fairy tales, Vi," Ford says, his voice dripping with disdain. "Get over this obsession with the five of us. Growing up means moving on. And sometimes friendships don't last."

"If you value them, you figure it out," she says, her voice wobbling.

"I guess I don't value this as much as you do," Ford says. Then, after a long look at Whitney, he walks out the door.

Violet collapses on the couch.

"Sully," Dani says quietly. "It's hurricane season. Maybe you should wait a couple months before heading out."

Sully turns back to face the group. "Nah. I need to go."

"But—" Violet begins.

Sully holds up a hand. "I'm going. I'll be okay."

He pauses halfway to the door and turns to me. "You're welcome to my boards while I'm gone. Come out to my truck, and I'll get you the key to the shed."

After a quick glance at Violet, I follow him out the door.

VIOLET

"Shit" is all I have to say when only Dani and Whitney and I are left.

"What the fuck, Whit? What were you thinking?" Dani asks.

"I wasn't, obviously," she says, swiping a hand across her cheek impatiently. "I've been going through some stuff with my parents, and I just thought we could go out quick and get a pack of cigarettes and be back before the storm hit."

"I mean, with what you said to the guys. You can't? You can't what?"

I don't mean to pile on but when Whitney just presses her lips together, I can't help but add, "You can't choose? Come on, Whit. That's just bullshit, and you know it."

Dani begins to pace in front of the fireplace. "You have got to get over this needing everybody to like you crap. Sometimes you have to make a choice, even if someone's going to be mad at you. Once you do, then people can actually get over it and move on."

"I-I don't mean to—" Whitney begins.

"You blew this group wide open seven years ago, and now you've done it again. And you know what? I'm done." Dani stops moving, hands on her hips, and looks out the window. After a few beats, she adds. "I think you're going to have to find another place to live."

Her bottom lip trembling, Whitney nods and stumbles down the hall toward her room.

"Dani! Don't you think that was a little harsh? I'm sure she feels bad enough as it is."

She whirls to launch her anger at me. "Her parents coddle her, and we baby her. She'll never be able to stand on her own two feet if someone doesn't kick her out of the nest."

"I get what you're saying, but I get the feeling that there's something—"

"It's okay, Vi," Whitney interrupts me from the doorway. Shouldering an oversized tote bag, she nods at me before turning to Dani. "You're right. I need to move on too. Just leave me a message when's a good time for me to stop by and pick up the rest of my things. I don't want to cause any more ruckus."

No one says a word, not even Nate, who holds the screen door as she exits.

When he replaces her in the doorway, Dani flicks a hand at me. "Y'all go on. I need some time."

I've never heard Dani's voice so hard. "Are we okay?"

"Yeah. I'm just… tired," she says on a sigh. "It's been a long couple of days."

Nate holds out a hand. "Come on, Vi. I'll drive you home."

Neither of us says anything as he steers his car toward the inn. It's only minutes away, but it feels like hours as the fight I just witnessed—possibly provoked—replays in my mind.

"I hope…" Nate begins. "I hope my being there didn't make things worse."

"Me too. But don't blame yourself. Maybe Ford is right. Maybe I've been living in dreamland trying to keep my friends close."

"There's nothing wrong with how you care about people," Nate says, his voice rough with emotion. "You're doing your best to be a good friend, a good person."

"How do you know? You barely know me," I argue.

"There's no bullshit behind what you do or say. You're doing the best you can."

"I guess sometimes that's just not enough." I rub my temples, where a headache is building. "It's just so damn frustrating. It's like we can't get out of this pattern where the guys run away and the girls are left to try to pick up the pieces."

"Give them time to cool down. It may take longer than you want, but it's clear your roots are deep." He stops in front of the inn instead of pulling into the driveway. "You may be able to repair bridges eventually."

"Do you not want to come in?"

"I didn't want to assume."

"I'd like company, but I'll have to warn you, I may not be up for more than whatever's on TV."

"That'd be fine with me. How about I head back to the hotel and pick up some dinner on the way back? I'll bring a

KAREN GREY

change of clothes for tomorrow, too, so we won't have to rush around in the morning."

I nod. It's nice to have someone who's willing to change their life around to accommodate mine for a change. "That sounds perfect."

I open the car door but hesitate before my foot hits the pavement. "I don't think I can take any more fighting. Whatever you and I need to do to work out things down at the studio, I'll do it."

"That sounds like a good plan. I have some ideas about that."

"Which we can discuss tomorrow. At work. Not tonight."

"Even better."

I lean across the console to give him a grateful kiss. The moment we touch, it's like slipping into a warm bubble bath. Sensual and relaxing all at once. I know it won't last. Passion cools, just like water does in a tub. For now, I'll take the distraction.

He eventually breaks the kiss to hold the sides of my face, his touch tender. "To be continued. I'll be back."

"I'll be here," I say before floating up the driveway and up the stairs to my apartment, determined to hold onto this feeling of peace as long as I can. All the messes in my life can wait until tomorrow.

CHAPTER 12

Lawson's Reach, "Boyfriend"

Jill makes an important decision about her relationship with Lawson.

VIOLET

The only way I got through the following week was to compartmentalize. Every single thing in my life is either in disarray or is totally up in the air. It used to be that I'd get a zing of satisfaction when I'd get through a day and every item on my to-do list was ticked off, even though it was impossibly long to start with.

Of course, I used to have time with my friends to look forward to at the end of a long day. Whether it was a bonfire at the beach or a cookout at Dani's, it's been awesome to relive our youth for the past few months. Now, Ford and Sully have taken off and Whitney isn't answering my calls. I see Dani briefly when we trade off Skye—at least the schedule is easy now that it's down to just two of us—but she doesn't stay or ask if I want to hang out.

I do have Nate, but between my long days and his getting settled at his new place, I haven't seen much of him outside the gates of the studio lot. Not that I've seen much of anything outside of the lot. Even walks with Skye are doubled up with picking up coffee or a meal, every one of which I eat at my desk.

Nate's spent a couple nights at my place this week, but they haven't exactly been restful for me. Part of it was staying up late for lovemaking, but part of it was lying awake wondering what we're doing. Are we dating? How long is he staying in town? He hasn't brought any of it up, so I don't want to ask and come off as clingy.

I just like to know what to expect.

Meanwhile, I may have softened toward the man himself, but his family's choices continue to be a thorn in my side. Calls to producer contacts have netted me background jobs, but Nate's dad has already scooped up all the local casting. The problem is, casting extras is not only less rewarding than filling day-player roles, but you also get less buck for your bang. There's an awful lot of running around and running people down, yet the production company pays less for it. I'm doing okay money-wise, but I would've been doing so much better without interference from Alan Fowler.

To make things worse, actor friends continue to stop by to complain about Nate. And it's not just that they don't know him. Even the most experienced of them are flummoxed by the way he runs a session. Not all casting directors give direction or coaching, but each and every actor who comes crying to me claims that he's impatient and rushes them through like he wishes he were anywhere else.

Thing is, I'm not sure I can just say, *Hey, now that we're having sex, I need to tell you that you suck at your job.* It does make me wonder: Why is he even doing this if he hates it so much?

My thoughts are interrupted by a ringing phone, as usual.

Later, I'm on what seems like the thousandth call of the morning when Mrs. Wilson and Nate walk in my office. I hold up a finger indicating that I'll be with them in a moment, but something about their expressions has me concerned, so I finish up my call quickly. "You know you're always at the top of my list, Mr. Fearrington. You just let me know when you're feeling better."

After I hang up I explain, "He really is the best background guy I have. So friendly. Everyone loves him."

"Is he alright?" Mrs. Wilson asks.

"He will be. He just has to have a kidney stone removed." I shake my head. "He was so embarrassed to tell me about it."

Mrs. Wilson nods. "I'll put out the word, and we'll make sure he has some meals brought over. And a ride to the appointment."

"That would be great. I was wondering how he'd deal with that." I look back and forth between them, but before I can ask what they need, the phone rings again. "Casting Carolina, can you hold please?"

I gesture at the piles on my desk and the blinking light on the phone. "I'm afraid I don't have much time to chat."

"We'll get right to it, then, because that's why we're here," Nate says. "Betty has been concerned that we get a number of calls from extras looking for work—that is, people who really need to speak to you."

"I give out your number fourteen-point-three times a day, on average," she says. "Additionally, your phones ring thirty-five percent more often than ours do."

"You added it up?" I ask.

"It's not just addition, dear. There are other formulas involved." She frowns. "Did you not take statistics?"

"I took it, but I didn't exactly get an A."

She sighs, but before she can lay into me about my lack of mathematical skills, Nate's hand goes up. "Regardless of how we got to the diagnosis, we think we have a solution."

My phone rings again, and I give them a tight smile. I pick up and get the person's name and number, promising to call them right back. I do the same with the person on hold. "I'm ready to hear your idea. Obviously, the thirty-five percent is getting to me."

He points to a phone jack in the wall that separates our offices. "We have a jack in the same spot, so it would be easy to run a few lines through. That would allow Betty to answer the phone for both businesses."

I'm having a hard time picturing this. "And then what? She'd, like, knock three times on the ceiling if she wants me?"

Nate snorts, obviously picking up on my reference to the old 70s song.

Mrs. Wilson, on the other hand, ignores the joke. "I would triage the calls. If they are simple requests for information, I can give that out. I can do intake for anyone seeking to be added to your roster, whether that's in person or on the phone."

"But what about the name difference? Won't that be confusing?"

"It's already confusing, dear. I'll just answer 'Casting' and be done with it."

One line after another lights up on my phone. I'm tired enough to give on this. "Fine. Great. Thank you." I wave at the wall. "Do whatever you need to do. I'm obviously drowning here."

"I'll get right to it," Nate says with a smile, seeming happy to have helped out.

"And we'll work out how to split Mrs. Wilson's salary?" I ask. I can't afford to hire an assistant of my own, but I'm not a charity case, either.

"We can talk about that tonight," Nate says. When Mrs. Wilson's brows go up, he adds, "Over dinner. A dinner meeting."

"Sounds good." Not sure why he's hiding the fact that we are doing whatever we're doing, I give him a tight smile before picking up the phone. "Casting Carolina, what can I do for you?"

NATE

At the end of my workday, Violet is still going strong. My family's business never handled extras casting, so I didn't realize how much work it takes. Still, the way Violet does it seems to take more time than is necessary. When she agreed to go out to dinner with me tonight, I made a reservation for seven, thinking that'd give her enough time to finish. But she's still going strong at 6:45, so I go back to my office and change the reservation to eight.

Since her friend group imploded, she's also had Skye more often, so in between phone calls I offer to take the dog for a walk around the lot. Her grateful smile is all the reward I need, but the way she gives all her energy to her job is still worrisome to me.

When we're in bed, our bodies act like we've known each other forever and would trust each other with our lives. But I have no idea what she wants from me beyond that, and every time I've gotten up the courage to try to talk about it, she's rushed off to the office or to check in extras or to help her grandparents. And there's no pillow talk after sex; she's asleep by the time I get back from throwing away the condom.

The fact that it'd be a close race between her and my dad in a workaholic contest should be a blaring cause for concern. He's never slowed down for me, so why should I expect that she would?

I'd hoped for a romantic meal at sunset when I made dinner reservations at the Riverboat Landing, with its picturesque little balconies overlooking the Cape Fear river, but I'll have to be satisfied with getting the woman alone for an hour without the distractions of a ringing phone.

Downtown Wallington closes up at night, except for the bars. In fact, on our way to the restaurant, we pass by the Ice House, a place that always seems to have a band playing in its half-inside, half-outside setup.

"Dani told me they're going to add that place as a regular location," Violet says. "A couple of the characters are going to work there."

"That'll require a lot of background, I suppose."

"It will," she says with a heavy sigh.

I put an arm around her shoulders. "Sorry. I didn't mean to bring up work."

"Isn't this a work dinner? I thought we were going to talk about sharing Mrs. Wilson."

"I said that, but I was hoping we could have a romantic meal first," I say as I open the door to the restaurant.

"If I have a glass of wine, I'll be out like a light," she warns.

Once we're settled at a table on the balcony, she does seem to relax as she takes in the view. "I've never actually eaten at this place."

"Really? Is the food not good?"

She shakes her head as she peruses the menu. "The kind of guys I've dated were more into the bar we just passed. This place'd be way out of their price range. And mine."

The waitress arrives to take our orders, and we both go for the shrimp and grits, which the place is famous for. Then I make a proposal. "How about we get the business talk out of the way, and then we can relax?"

She frowns.

"Or whatever you want. Food first, then work." I reach for her hand. "I just want to be able to enjoy time with you."

"Do you not enjoy your work, Nate?"

I sit back in my chair, a bit thrown by her question. "I enjoy some of what I'm doing, but… it's work."

She looks out over the river. "That day at Masonboro. You said, 'All work and no play makes Jack a dull boy.' Do you think I'm dull?"

There's an edge to her tone that worries me, but maybe it's time to be honest about my concerns. "I was thinking about my dad that day. He *never* stops working. When I was a kid, the only time I spent with him was at his office. Even the weekends he had us after the divorce—most of which he begged off of because he was 'too busy'—he was either dragging us off to some event where he was all about schmoozing people or I was sitting in a dark room all day running the camera for auditions or workshops."

"And you hated that?"

"I was a kid. A boy who loved running around outside. So yeah, I hated it. Do you blame me for wanting my dad to go to my Little League game instead of watching stupid actors read the same damn lines over and over again?"

"The thing is, I love the work I'm doing. It's important to me to do it well. And to not rely on anyone else." She looks out over the water again. "In fact—"

The waitress arrives with the half carafe of wine we ordered. After she pours it and disappears again, I raise my glass and catch her gaze. "How about this? We split Betty's salary fifty-fifty. Having her answer both phones is really more efficient all around. I'm not doing this just to help you out."

She presses her lips together for a moment, like she's keeping herself from arguing, but thankfully, she nods and clinks glasses with me. "That sounds like a fair deal."

VIOLET

After we get back in his car after dinner, Nate asks, "Would you like to come see my new place?"

So many questions run through my mind in response that my brain stalls. From worry about the state of my business to wondering about where things stand between us, I can't seem to come up with a response.

"It's a simple yes or no question," he says with a sigh.

"Is it?" I snap.

"I'm not the enemy, you know," he says, exasperation coloring his tone. "I'm not my father, and I can't be responsible for his machinations. Or whatever his problem with my uncle is."

"I get that, I just wish you weren't—"

"Here?"

"Not exactly. I enjoy you being here. Most of the time."

"Most of the time?"

"You know what I mean. There are so many issues between us. I guess I wish you—"

"Had a fishing supply business? So we could trade signs?"

He scores a laugh from me, but just barely. "That would make things simpler."

He twists a finger into one of my curls and tugs gently. "And then I could use my rod to reel you in?"

After a groan I concede, "I think you've already done that."

Releasing my hair, he scoops up my hand, which feels small in his. "Look, I don't want to pressure you. If you want me to take you home, just say so. Or if you need to pick up Skye—"

"No, that's not it. Dani has her tonight. I'm just feeling a little overwhelmed." I blow out a breath to try and release some pent-up tension. "I would like to see your place. I'll just have to get up and go home in the morning."

"To work? It's Saturday."

"Yeah. I have to help Gran do the turnover, and then I have classes to teach."

He shakes his head, and his brow furrows. "More hours indoors. With actors."

"If you're going to judge how I spend my time, maybe you should take me home."

"I'm sorry," he says, releasing my hand and rubbing his own over his forehead. "I don't mean to ruin what little time we have together."

Whether he's talking about his limited time in Wallington or my limited time because I work so much, either one gets my hackles up. "That *is* what you're doing, though. Complaining about how I choose to live my life every chance you get. Maybe it's what you did with your dad."

"What do you mean?"

"If you were grumpy when he took you places, maybe that's why he avoided doing it."

"I was a kid," he says, his tone sharp. "He was the adult."

"I'm sorry." Hand up between us, I back off. "You're right."

"Look, let's just—" he begins.

"Maybe we should—" I say at the same time.

"You go first," he says.

A cleansing breath only gets me halfway under control. I don't like that he pushes my buttons, and yet, in bed, that same button pushing makes me lose control in all the good ways. Perhaps real passion has a price I'm not used to paying. "I was going to suggest we start over. I would like to see your place."

"And I would like to get naked with you. And make you forget about work."

"Challenge accepted."

His place is only minutes away, in the historic part of downtown where many of the old turn-of-the-century homes have been cut up into apartments. He gives me the five-minute tour, and I admire the mullioned windows and crown molding before he turns his attention to making me forget about anything and everything beyond the confines of his bed.

As he has every time we're alone, he reels me in, just as promised. Even my stubborn frontal lobe rolls over to play dead when his strong hands grab my ass. When he hikes me up to straddle his hips like I weigh nothing. When his erection grinds into my needy center.

"There is way too much fabric between us," I groan.

"Easy fix." He eases me back down to my feet while continuing to hold me close, the friction lighting little fires of desire as I slide down his body. Then, growling and giggling with impatience, we fumble with buttons and zippers.

Finally freed of my clothing, I try to leap onto the high four-poster bed, but end up sprawled on my belly. "That was graceful," I snort.

"Gives me an excellent view."

Peeking at him from under my hair, I ask, "See anything you like, sir?"

He just shakes his head, his beautiful mouth spreading slowly into a camera-ready smile. "I want everything on this menu. I don't know where to start."

His hands slip under my torso to squeeze my breasts, then sweep around to glide down my back again and knead my butt cheeks. I arch into his touch before rolling onto my back and reaching for him with both hands.

He clambers all the way up on the bed, as lacking in grace as myself, before rolling us both so that I'm straddling him. Hands braced on either side of his perfect face, I sink down until my breasts spread over his pecs as my mouth finds his.

Lost in the kiss, all my worries float away. Maybe being my own boss isn't all that important. Naked together, we trade being in charge effortlessly. I take what I want and give when I want, and he does the same.

There's one niggling worry left—the fact that his presence here isn't permanent, that he could up and leave me anytime —but I've dealt with that before, and I'll do it again. For now, his lips on mine are all I want to think about. Ticking items off a to-do list or telling an actor he got the job may make me happy.

But when I let go of everything and just feel with this man… that brings me pure bliss.

CHAPTER 13

LAWSON'S REACH, "BOYFRIEND"
PARKER ACCIDENTALLY PICKS A FIGHT WITH CHARLI.

NATE

GETTING TO THE BEACH EVERY MORNING ISN'T QUITE AS EASY when I'm no longer staying steps away from the ocean, and without Sully it's not quite as fun. Still, I don't want his storage locker full of boards to go to waste. I even made some new buddies on this morning's dawn patrol. One told me about a beach cleanup he's organized over the weekend, and the other invited me to hear his band play this evening.

Hoping that having Betty help out will mean that Violet has more time for fun, I head over to invite her to check out this guy's music with me. When I open the door to her office, however, I hear two voices I recognize. One is Violet's, but the other is a guy that I just taped for a speaking role in an indie film that Fowler Stern is casting. My dad will sometimes do smaller films in return for a producer credit as well as a cut of the profits. If there are any. He's only putting his time and name down in return, so it does seem to be a good way to increase the bottom line in the long run.

It's not that that has me stopping in my tracks, however. It's what the actor is saying. "I feel like everything I've been working on the past five years just goes out the window when I go in that room."

"You can't let it get to you," Violet says in a soothing tone.

"Which part? The part where the guy ruins my chances of getting the job because he's so impatient to get things over with—like I'm there to pull his teeth instead of turn in a performance—that he turns off the camera before I've even finished the scene? Or the part where he practically bites my head off when I ask to do another take? Or the part where he taps his watch like I've taken up too much of his time already?"

Violet murmurs something in response, but then I hear her chair shift and her voice gets louder, like she's walking him toward the door. "You just have to do the work and let all that roll off your back. I wish I could talk more, but I've got extras to call."

I step out into the hallway and duck into the copy room before they see me. The room is empty, the only sounds the humming of the machines, and their words echo in my head, making my face heat with shame. Am I really that bad at this? There's not exactly a school where you can study to be a casting director. I figured running the camera for my dad's casting workshops for more Saturdays than I can count was as good a preparation as one could get. I frame them up and make sure the lighting is good. I edit the tape and get it to the director as efficiently as possible, even from the other side of the country.

But I have no idea what I'm doing—or not doing, as the case may be—that's making these actors so uncomfortable, so I have no idea how to fix it. I have a feeling who might, however, and I'll just have to be man enough to ask her.

151

When I return to Vi's office, I find her at her desk with a typed list in front of her—not printed out, mind you, but typed on an old word processor. There are checkmarks next to a few of the names and scrawled notes in the margins.

From the all-caps header on the page—the title of the indie movie we're working on, plus tomorrow's date—it's clear that she's contacting background actors to give them their call times. But instead of doing that, she's asking about someone's dog.

"I heard she had puppies! How many were there?" She nods, listening patiently to whatever the caller is going on about, even though she's got a long list of names in front of her. Thinking that some friend must have called, I lean against the door to wait until she's finished.

Finally, she wraps it up. "Give her a pat for me. And we'll see you tomorrow morning at six o'clock sharp. Casual clothes, like you're going to a ballgame. Bring a couple different color shirts, just in case. Bye now."

Before I can ask if she wants to get dinner, she dials again. When the person answers, she wastes a ridiculous amount of time chatting with them about some event happening downtown. On the next call, she asks the person how their mom is doing. When she hangs up, I close the space between the doorway and her desk to put a finger on the switch hook before she can dial again.

She yelps, which has Skye on her feet and barking. Hand to her heart, Violet says, "Jesus! You scared the shit out of me. I thought you were long gone."

"How do you know all that stuff about all those people?" I'd meant to point out the inefficiency in her methodology, but I suppose I'm more curious about how her brain works, since it's clearly nothing like mine.

"It's all up here." She taps a finger to her temple. "Little details about their lives help me remember them."

She looks pointedly at my fingers depressing the knobs on

the telephone, but I don't move. "It takes you ten minutes to call each person. Why do you do that? Why not just tell them what time to show up and leave it at that? In fact, why not set up the answering machine with an outgoing message that tells them the time and place?"

"Because then they might *not* show up."

"If they don't, don't hire them again. They're the ones that need you. You're the one with the jobs."

"Honey," she says, but the tone under the endearment is more sour than sweet. "This is not a job anyone does for the fifty bucks they get. They do this because it's fun. I mean, I have a couple of people who do need the money. But most of them, it's so they can tell their friends they're going to be on TV or in a movie—"

"Exactly. They need you."

She doesn't even bother to argue with my words, she just sweeps them away with her hand as she continues. "Most of all? It's civic pride. But whatever their motivation, it's a lot to get people excited about spending twelve hours waiting around, often in less-than-comfortable circumstances. Charming them is part of the job."

I want to say to her what I wanted to say to my dad: *Your charm is wasted on them. You need to take better care of yourself. Working long hours is bad for your health. You need to laugh and enjoy the fresh air. You need to pay attention to* me. But before I can, she waves a hand in my face.

"Did you need something? Because I have more calls to make. And I'll be checking in these folks tomorrow morning, so I'd like to be able to go home and go to bed at some point."

Even the thought that she might be going to bed with me doesn't stop my mouth. "This could be done so much more efficiently. We've got more phone lines. I'll set up a dedicated actor hotline and a separate machine. We could record a series of options, and every day Betty could update it with new casting opportunities as well as call times. Then you wouldn't have to make all these damn phone calls and stay here till god knows when."

Her nostrils flare as she pushes my hand out of the way and sets the receiver on the phone. "Just because you have contracted work out to me, just because we are having sex, does not mean you get to tell me how to run my business."

The way she says "having sex" like it's not something she's looking forward to pricks my pride. "Fine. You waste your life away at work then. Spend all your time inside these faux-paneled walls."

Standing, she stares me down. "When I agreed to take on this work, I said it had to be on my terms. Believe me, I'd rather be auditioning people for speaking roles, but this is the work that I've ended up doing because of your goddamn family feud, so leave me the hell alone so I can do it."

This has my temper flaring, even as I realize that it's really my dad I've been talking to.

Before I can explain that, she points at the door. "Now."

"Vi, I—"

"Nate, you need to leave before I get even more pissed off at you."

"Okay, I'm leaving." I back toward the door, but as she begins to dial, I whisper, "Can this be the kind of lovers' spat where we make up later and have makeup sex?"

She rolls her eyes. "Instead of a battle between mortal enemies where I tell you to leave and never come back?"

"Yes?"

She just waves a hand at me and picks up the phone. After I close the door softly behind me, kicking myself for losing my temper, she yells, "It better be some damn good makeup sex!"

VIOLET

After I make the last phone call of the night, all I want to do is go back to my apartment, have a glass of wine, and go to bed. But there's a man out there waiting to have makeup sex with me.

And a dog back at my apartment waiting to be let out.

If I'm honest with myself, time with both of them will make me happy. So I call Nate, ask if he'll meet me at my place, and then head home. Once there, I toss my bag on the floor, put a leash on Skye, and take her out to sniff around and do her business.

When Nate shows up, she barks at him fiercely *and* wags her tail. Kind of how I feel.

"I come in peace!" he says, holding up a couple of shopping bags. "And I bring gifts."

"What kind of gifts?" I ask as Skye sniffs eagerly at one of the bags.

"That's right, this is for you, girl," he says, pulling a dog toy out of the bag. "You fill this with treats. I thought it might keep her busy while we… you know."

"What about me? What's going to get me in the mood to 'you know'?"

Hand to his chest, he gasps theatrically. "I never noticed you needing anything to get in the mood before."

"Yeah, well, some guy at work put me in a pretty ugly frame of mind today."

"Really? What a jerk."

"Seriously."

"Good thing I brought wine, potato chips, and chocolate then."

"Hm," I sniff, hiding my delight as best I can. "I guess you can come in."

Inside the apartment, he stuffs treats into the dog toy while I open the wine.

155

"It's usually a tough call between alcohol, salt, and sugar, but today my choice is clear. All three." Opening the fancy bar of chocolate first, I take a big bite. "Unh. This is so good."

I set the candy down to get wine glasses. When I turn around, Nate's breaking off a piece of chocolate. "Hey! That's my mood booster."

He smirks. "Calm down. I don't like chocolate, remember?"

"Then why are you eating mine?"

"I was planning to feed it to you," he says as he folds the wrapper over the end of the bar. "But if you don't want me to—"

I growl in frustration. "Get over here and kiss me, you."

After a quick glance over his shoulder at Skye, clearly occupied by her own treat, he steps close to do just that.

"Mmm. Want more," I murmur between kisses.

"More kisses or more chocolate?" he asks.

"More of everything."

"Your wish is my command."

After taking my wine glass and setting it next to his on the counter, he slides one hand across my back and the other behind my knees and picks me up before I know what's happening.

When I yelp in surprise, Skye barks.

"I'm fine, sweet girl," I call.

"Pick up your treats," Nate orders.

"Are you talking to me or the dog?"

When he growls in response, I grab the chocolate and shove it in my cleavage, tuck the bag of chips between my teeth, and then pick up the two glasses of wine.

"Good girl." Again, his words could be for Skye or me, but it's me that he carries into the bedroom. After he kicks the door shut behind him, he says, "Just don't want to traumatize the poor dog while Mommy and Daddy get it on."

He carries me close to the bedside table so I can set

down the glasses and the chips. He tosses me onto the bed as I'm retrieving the chocolate. Fumbling it as I land, it falls on the bed beside me. Before I can grab it, he pounces, swinging a leg over my hips. "You're going to have to work for it."

I wiggle underneath his pelvis. "My pleasure."

As he breaks off a piece of chocolate, I cup his hard length and squeeze. With each stroke, he feeds me another bite of chocolate. By the time the bar is gone, he's moaning my name in pleasure.

I scoot out of my dress as he rolls on a condom. He strips off my underthings while I reach for a bottle of lube in my bedside drawer. His methodical and thorough application has me writhing with need. Between his touch and the heat of the lotion, my pump is primed as much as his.

"Mm," he murmurs against my lips. "So much goodness."

I arch into him as he plunges inside. When he circles his hips, I grip him with my vaginal walls, eliciting a guttural groan.

He meets my gaze, his grin wicked. "I want to watch you touch yourself."

"Happy to oblige," I say. Dribbling more of the liquid on my nipples, I circle them until they peak.

"Squeeze them," he orders. "Pinch them hard."

"Like this?" I ask, breathy with need, desire building.

"Like that," he says, pushing deeper. "And now your pussy. I want you to make yourself come while I'm inside."

I like this bossy side of Nate.

"Do you?"

"Whoops. Didn't mean to say that out loud."

"I'm glad you like it. I've never said things like this before, but… you make me so fucking horny, so hot with wanting to fuck you, I… I want you to feel the same."

His fierce revelation makes me even wilder with need, so I reach for the Butter Bean and begin to circle. Faster and harder as I get closer and closer to the edge, as my entire body clenches around my heated center.

As he strokes in and out, the hand not braced on the headboard palms my breast. I join him with my free hand until I'm overwhelmed with sensation. "I'm coming," I whisper.

"Keep going, baby," he says. "I want to feel you."

When I let go, his thrusts extend my orgasm and its aftershocks until he goes over the edge with a roar.

"Fuuuck," he groans before collapsing on top of me.

NATE

We're still breathing hard from sex that, unbelievably, just keeps getting more intense, when I open mouth to insert foot. "I thought you didn't like being told what to do."

The slap to my butt is hard and instantaneous.

"I deserved that," I admit.

"Yes, you did."

She shifts next to me and leans across my back briefly. When I roll to my side to face her, she's sitting up against the headboard, calmly sipping wine, so I join her.

Looking straight ahead, she says, "I started Casting Carolina because I want to work for myself, be my own boss."

"I have no issue with that," I say after thinking about it for a few moments. "I just don't want to spend my whole life working. I want to be on the water, be outside."

She looks over at me. "Do I keep you from doing that?"

When I shake my head she asks, "Do I make you feel bad about it?"

"You don't make me feel bad, but…" I pause to choose my words carefully because I want to make sure I'm really talking about what's going on between us. "I think, because of my history with my dad—of him always choosing work over me—it felt like you were doing the same when I made a suggestion that would save you time."

Eyes narrowing slightly, she counters, "When you made that suggestion, it felt to me like you were judging me. Like I was doing it the stupid way and you knew a better way."

I really have to bite my tongue because that is what I think.

"That is what you think, isn't it?"

"No, not that you're doing it the *stupid* way. It's more that… I just don't get why you'd choose to do something so inefficiently."

She takes another sip of wine and stares across the room for a few moments. "I do think there are some things I could do more efficiently. And I would be interested in hearing your ideas on the subject. But I think it should happen at a specified time. Like, we have a company meeting every once in a while to discuss ideas."

"I think that's a good idea. We shouldn't try and make changes when we're tired or stressed." Words from the conversation I overheard earlier between her and the disgruntled actor echo in my head. "But I know I would like to hear your thoughts about how I could improve at running auditions. I feel like there are ways I could improve."

She looks over at me, like she can't wait to tell me all of her thoughts on the subject.

My hand goes up between us. "But not when you're angry and not right now."

She wrinkles her nose. "Should we just never talk about work in bed?"

"Betty says never say never."

"Well, if Mrs. Wilson says it…" She downs the rest of her wine before setting the glass on the bureau next to the bed.

"Don't be ragging on Betty."

"I won't rag on her if you promise to never bring her up when we're in bed again. And yes, I said never. Bite me."

I nuzzle behind her ear. "That's an order I can follow."

"As long as you promise to bite me and not talk about Betty… we're good." She rolls over to kiss me on the nose. "Got to go pee. And let Skye pee too."

After throwing on a robe, she disappears through the bedroom door. When I hear her go outside with the dog, I visit the bathroom to wash up and brush my teeth with the toothbrush she so thoughtfully laid out for me the first night I slept over.

My dad never did that, I realize. Didn't even occur to him, I bet.

When she and Skye come back in, I'm filling glasses of water for the both of us. After we climb back into bed, I roll over to face her again.

"What?" she asks.

"I could never get my dad to pay attention to me. I never believed he cared about me more than he cared about work— still don't. No matter what I do here, no matter how hard I try, I don't think that's going to change."

"I'm sorry."

Needing to touch her, I brush a tendril of hair away from her brow. "But it's not fair to assume that of you, because you don't treat me the same way he does. I'm going to try and remember that from now on."

She nods, but her gaze remains on the ceiling. "At least yours was around."

"Jeez. I'm an idiot," I totally forgot that her parents are dead. "I'm sorry."

When she doesn't say anything further, I ask, "How old were you when you lost your parents?"

"Puh. More like they lost me. They parked me with Gran and Pops when I was five and never came back."

Before I can ask what that means, she continues. "Or rather, they come back on the rare occasions where they're not 'stuck' in a 'remote location' that it's 'impossible' to get back from." Her tone sharpens with each set of air quotes.

But I can hardly blame her. Maybe our circumstances are more alike than I'd thought. "From the way you talked about them, I thought they'd passed away. They chose work over you too?"

"Yep. They get so caught up in what they're doing—and each other—that they forget I exist."

"I'm sorry."

"I'm luckier than a lot of kids," she says, sounding like she feels the opposite. "Gran and Pops were great. Are great."

"Still, it sucks to have your parents do that to you." When she doesn't say anything else, I ask, "How often do you see them?"

"It varies. But I haven't seen them in… two years, I think?"

"Two years? Where the hell are they?"

"Brazil."

"Doing what?"

"Building shit." She shrugs and flicks a hand like she doesn't really care. "They're engineers who specialize in buildings that can be built quickly and taken down quickly and can survive extreme weather in remote areas—temporary operations while a company creates a permanent home. It's pretty intense. They're pretty intense."

"You don't ever visit?"

"They don't want me to. It's too dangerous. I'd be distracting. I'd be bored." She ticks off each excuse on a finger. "They always have a reason."

"Did you *ever* travel with them?"

"They tried. At first, my mom didn't work after I was born, but then I guess she got really depressed, so she went back to work and brought me along. Then I got sick and almost died because they couldn't get to a doctor fast enough, so after that I stayed with my grandparents. They come home for a few months between jobs, but it's always awkward. Honestly, it feels like my grandparents are my real parents. Those people just spawned me.

"Anyway, that's why I need my friends so much. All of us have a different flavor of fucked-up family, so we kind of created our own."

"You're lucky."

"I am. Or I was."

She reaches over to turn off the bedside lamp, but not before I see the tear trickling down her cheek. I'm sure she doesn't want me to see this sign of what she probably thinks is weakness, so I don't say anything about it. What I do instead is scoot right up next to her to spoon her from behind.

Honored that she trusted me with a bit of her truth, I breathe with her until it feels like she's fallen asleep. And then I let myself follow.

CHAPTER 14

Lawson's Reach, "The Scare"

It's Friday the 13th, and no one is ready for what happens.

NATE

Every other morning that I've woken up next to Vi, she's been curled into a ball on her own side of the bed. When my eyes flutter open the day after she tells me about her parents, she's curled into my side instead. It feels more precious than I could've imagined.

It's still dark out, so I relax into her warmth until the first fingers of dawn begin to break through the slits of her shutters, and then I ease my arm out from under her. Vi doesn't need to get up for a couple hours, but I'm wide awake and pulled to the ocean. I write her a note and slip out the door, promising to return with coffee after I get in some much-needed time on my board.

Or rather, on one of Sully's boards. Since he left, I've made a few new friends, but I miss the guy. And I worry about him. I'm sure he knows what he's doing, having grown up around boats and the water, but heading out solo in a sailboat has got to be risky.

Once I'm out on the water myself, I do my best to emulate his Zen approach to surfing, guiding my meandering thoughts back to the waves and the wind, but it's not easy. Violet plays a starring role in most of my mental wanderings. Now that we're sleeping together more nights than not, I'm able to act on the sexual fantasies she's inspired from the day we met. But now other fantasies intrude. Ones that involve building a life with her.

I've also got less pleasant distractions. My sister called yesterday, actually reaching me on my cell phone. The thing that rings so seldom I usually forget I have it. But I answered yesterday and immediately wished I hadn't. I mean, I knew my dad's sixtieth birthday was coming up, but I figured any celebration would be like the rest of his social life.

Work-oriented. An excuse to schmooze.

Instead, my sister has arranged a family-only dinner and purchased a ticket for me to fly home. Since all of my work comes from projects she's actively working on or is supervising, she knows my schedule.

I have no excuses. But I really don't want to go.

For the first time in my life, I feel like I belong.

Not in my family, as I'd hoped to prove by coming here.

But here in Wallington. With Violet, in this town. The problem is, I can't see any way out of the current mess that won't create an even bigger rift between my father and me.

Which begs another question: Do I even care?

When Violet told me about her parents yesterday, I was outraged. They may have made sure she had her basic needs met over the years, but it their emotional contribution was... nonexistent.

Which is essentially what my dad did. He (mostly) fulfilled his legal duties by taking me and my sister (mostly) every other weekend. He paid for our schooling and the clothes on our backs.

But emotionally? He treated us like interns. Someone to fetch his coffee and do all the other scut work that he didn't want to pay anyone to do. If that intern is someone hoping to get a leg up in the business and learn the trade from the inside—something I'd like to talk to Violet about doing if we ever manage to schedule a company meeting—that's one thing. It's an entirely different deal if it's your kid.

My sister flourished in the environment. At least professionally. She's the backbone of the business. Her family life, on the other hand, needs work. She's great with the kids, but she and her husband seem to fight as much as our parents did.

Not that I'm an expert on making relationships work. With my parents' multiple examples, I figured people either got along and stayed married, or they didn't and divorced.

Every single thing about what's going on between Violet and me tells me that I was wrong. The woman drives me crazy—in good ways, in bad ways, and in all the ways in between. I've been angrier at her, hurt more by her, and—if I'm honest with myself—more in love with her than anyone I've ever known.

Every day with her is an adventure that I don't want to end. Which brings me back to the dilemma. Do I give up on pleasing my dad, quit the family business, and go to work for Violet instead? Would that even be possible?

A shout pierces the mental fog clouding my awareness of the here and now, but by the time I register the warning from a fellow surfer, it's too late to course-correct. The water I hadn't been paying attention to breaks right over my head, and I tumble off the board and into the hard-packed sand.

Luckily for me, the waves are relatively mellow today, so the damage is primarily to my ego. My elbow's got a nasty scrape and my butt's going to be sore later, but right now it's my head I've got to get on straight.

The only way I can figure to do that is to follow my heart.

VIOLET

Nate lets me sleep in when he slips out of bed early to go surfing. As I'm about to leave for work, he returns armed with coffee but with ugly cuts on his brow and elbow. I get him a Band-Aid and some Neosporin, and I don't say a word about how boneheaded I think surfing is. Like most kids who grow up here, I tried it. But between my fair skin and lack of coordination, I ended up with a sunburn that blistered and a concussion. That was the end of my surfing career in my grandmother's book.

Not that I minded. I'd rather sit under an umbrella and read if I'm going to the beach. Preferably with a cocktail.

But today, I need to butter my boyfriend up. There's a screening of a movie I worked on showing at Thalian Hall, just for local cast and crew. I don't usually bring a plus-one to what is essentially a work event, but I'd love to walk in with Nate on my arm. Thing is, we haven't exactly come out to the local show-biz public as a couple yet.

In fact, we still haven't defined what's going on between us, not to mention whether whatever that is has a chance of sticking and whether or not the show that pitted us against each other and brought us together will get renewed or not.

With all the unknowns, I decide I need all the backup I can get, so once we get to the studios, I stop by and snag him a slice of Randy's famous blueberry pie along with a large cup of coffee.

"What's your feeling about pie for breakfast?" I ask as I set them on Nate's desk.

"Ooh, is that blueberry?" He pulls the paper plate closer. "You obviously didn't tell Randy this was for me, otherwise the slice would be a quarter this size." He shovels a forkful into his mouth and moans appreciatively.

"Randy knows we don't hate each other anymore."

"Yeah," Nate says over a second mouthful. "That's a problem too. Now he hates me because he senses that we're together. He has a thing for you."

"He does not."

After putting his fork down, he pulls me over to sit on his lap. "You may have excellent people skills, but you've got a blind spot when it comes to guys who are into you. Which includes most men in town."

"Pshaw. That's ridiculous."

He shakes his head. "Not from what I've seen."

I put my arms around his neck and give him a kiss. "Well, you don't have to worry about the competition. They've had years to ask me out."

"I'm glad to hear it."

His berry-flavored lips find mine, and the kiss turns hot and heavy quickly—almost, but not quite, distracting me from my purpose. Breaking the kiss, I fork up another bite of pie and feed it to him, giving me a chance to make my ask.

"If you really are worried about losing me to other suitors in town, you should come along with me to an event this week."

His brows come together. "What kind of event? And when? Because you know I have to fly back to LA for my dad's birthday."

"A screening. Wednesday night. You'll still be here."

"A movie screening?" he asks, like I'd asked him to another kind of screening. The one where he'd have to bend over and cough. "God, I hate those. My dad was always dragging us to those things."

I stare him down. "As we have established, I am not your dad."

"But still," he whines. "I hate everything about them. Dressing up, schmoozing, paparazzi. Everybody prancing around trying to prove how important they are."

"Nate, Wallington is not LA. I don't know when you're going to figure that out. Not only do you not have to dress up, but if you make an effort to meet the local actors outside of this office, they won't be so intimidated by you. That's the opposite of trying to prove something. It's letting them see you're just another guy."

"Just another guy, huh?"

I give him a sweet kiss on the cheek. "Just another guy who wants to help his lady out by being her date."

He scrunches up his nose. "I really don't have to dress up?"

"Dude, you walked into this town in an Armani suit."

"I haven't missed wearing those things one bit."

"You can wear what you want to this thing. Nobody cares."

"Board shorts and a surf-shop tee?"

"What. Ever. You. Want."

"Okay. I'll go. But I'm not going to like it."

I just shake my head. "Thank you. I appreciate it."

"Show me how much you appreciate it?"

Hopping off his lap, I swipe the last bite of his pie. "Later. If you're lucky. Right now, somebody's got to get some work done around here."

It's five o'clock on a Friday afternoon. In August. For most people, even people who don't live at the beach, the work week would've ended hours ago. But as always, I'm the last one standing—or sitting, as the case may be—here at the production offices.

I used to love being here after hours. While the offices go dark, the stages never really rest. Even if nothing's shooting, there's always someone building a set or breaking one down. I'd take a tour and visit with other night owls when I needed a break.

But today, the AC's on the fritz and I'm counting the calls I have to make before I can go home.

Just as I check off number nineteen, Skye whines and wiggles her way toward the open door of my office. When I see who it is, I ask, "Hey Dani, what's up?"

She gives Skye a scratch under the chin. "Just seeing if you and our girl want to go for a W-A-L-K on the B-E-A-C-H."

Skye has a big vocabulary. If we say either of those words, she starts spinning and howling.

"Ugh. I'd love to, but I've got to make these calls."

Dani pushes out her lower lip in a pout. "Bummer. I feel like I haven't seen you in a while."

She was the one who said she wanted space a week ago, but I'm not going to throw that back at her. I miss her too much. "I'm sorry. Can we make a date?"

We're going through our calendars trying to find a time we're both free when Nate walks in with a hopeful grin on his face. "Are you finished for the day?"

"I am not, unfortunately."

"I am," Dani says. "Want to go to the B-E-A-C-H with the D-O-G and me?"

Nate looks to me for what seems to be permission so I shoo them towards the door. "Y'all go. Tire the pup out."

"I wish I could help you," he says. "See you later?"

"Actually, my grandparents said they need to talk to me about something, and I feel like I've been neglecting them lately."

He nods and then steps close to plant a kiss on my lips. Right in front of Dani. "See you later."

Dani gives me a *we-need-to-talk* look before the three of them walk out the door.

Leaving me alone with the phone and my goddamn lists.

NATE

As Dani and I walk to our cars, she asks, "I usually like to go to Carolina Beach with the dog. You okay with that?"

I shrug. "Sure. I've never been there."

"I figured you for a Wrightsford snob."

"I've never even heard of it."

"My point exactly."

"Hey, somebody at our offices in LA made the reservation at the Rumrunner. Then Sully showed me all the good surfing spots, which were all on that same island."

She just shakes her head. "It's a bit of a longer drive from here, but it's worth it. Crowds are smaller, and the dog can go off leash. A lot of folks around here call it the redneck beach, but maybe I'm a redneck, 'cause I like it. Plus, there's an excellent place we can stop to get a slice of pizza, and Britt's has the best donuts you'll ever eat."

"Pizza for dinner and donuts for dessert? I'm in. How about we go together? If I drive, I'll learn the way there. I can bring you back here afterwards."

"Sounds good to me."

During the twenty-minute drive, Dani manages to get me spilling all my secrets. Must be some kind of bartender trick. Before I know it, I'm telling her all about my family and how I don't fit in.

"No one gets me, they make fun of me, they criticize everything I do—"

"Isn't that what family does?" It's hard to tell if she's kidding or not.

"I guess, to a certain extent. But I'm like…"

"The black sheep?"

"Worse than that. It feels like they're indifferent. Unimpressed."

"Is that why you're here? Did you run away from home?"

"Actually, it's kind of the opposite. I tried to run away, working at a string of places after college. The kind of conglomerate with a name that makes it impossible to tell what exactly they do or make. Like Iliad Holdings or Gansett or Citimark."

"Did you do casting for them?"

"No, no. Well, kind of. I was in HR."

"Huh. So you were hiring people to make…"

"I didn't even know half the time, but that really wasn't the problem."

"What was the problem?"

"Well, I missed the ocean for sure. Most of the places were not on the coast."

"That'd be a dealbreaker for me."

"My family says that I run when I get bored. Which is partly true. But really, I hated the predictability of the job. The nine-to-five was killing me."

"Oh yes, it's much better working six to nine like we do. AM to PM."

"It wasn't the hours. It's more that I like change. Anyway, after I quit the last job and was back in LA looking for work, my sister asked me to fill in for the camera guy one day. I always hated my dad's business, but I wasn't busy, so I said yes."

"And you fell in love all over again?"

"Not exactly. It's more like none of the other offers I was getting seemed like a good fit, and my sister just kept getting me to sub in for this or that thing. And then—for the first time in my life—my dad was paying attention to me for something other than getting called to the principal's office."

"How'd you end up here?"

"My dad asked me to open this office and stay here through the summer. He made me commit to three months because, like I said, I have a reputation for moving on when things get boring."

"What's your plan with Vi?"

"She wasn't exactly part of the plan."

She points to the entrance of a parking lot. "We're here."

Once we let Skye out of the car, the dog requires all of our attention. There are a few other people with dogs, and Skye has a ball running around with them, splashing in and out of the surf.

As we walk along the beach watching Skye play and enjoying the sunset, Dani no longer asks question after question. Maybe she got the intel she was looking for.

Unfortunately, she's stirred up an unfamiliar unease for me. I've been reveling in the time I have with Violet without really thinking about what comes next. Originally, I'd planned to be here for the summer, maybe into the fall. But once I proved myself, I figured I'd go back to the main office for pilot season in January—the busiest time of the year for casting directors.

But not only are things different here than I expected, I'm not sure what it is I want anymore. Violet has changed that.

Dani interrupts my reverie by taking my hand and placing a small object in it.

"What's this?"

"Sea glass," she explains.

I lift the oblong object, which is not like any chunk of glass I've seen before. Not quite translucent, not quite transparent, it's sort of a cloudy white. Like an opal almost. It's irregular in shape, but there are no sharp edges. "Where did it come from?"

"If you have an eye for it, they're pretty easy to find in the sand." She gestures out at the water. "Bottles or whatever break, and out there, they get tumbled in the sand and waves until all their sharp edges are worn. Every day these babies wash up on shore with the shells and driftwood."

"Cool," I say, rubbing its surface with my hand.

When I try to hand it back to her, she shakes her head. "I've got piles of them at my house. That's for you. To remind you of your time here."

VIOLET

The entire time I'm phoning to give extras the time they need to show up tomorrow, I'm kicking myself. Yes, it's important for me to have a human connection with these people, but I can do that when I make the initial call to book them. I don't need to do it twice.

I would much rather be enjoying a twilight walk on the beach with Nate and Dani and Skye than sitting here making phone calls.

I'll just have to admit that he was right. Not my favorite thing to do, but when you're wrong, you're wrong.

It's past eight by the time I finish up, so my last call is to my grandparents to let them know I'm on the way. Gran's tone is odd but not like she has bad news, so I try to put worry to the side for the short trip home.

When I get there, there's a glass of fresh-squeezed lemonade and a plate of my grandfather's homemade cookies ready for me. They always used to put a treat out for me after school, and for some reason this makes me worried.

"Is everything okay?" I ask.

Gran sends a shifty look to my grandfather. "Everything's fine."

"Sit down, sweetheart. Take a load off," Pops says.

I look back and forth between them, trying to suss out what's going on. "Y'all are being weird."

He claps his hands together. "Well, we do have news."

"Just spit it out, then. You're making me nervous."

After a long pause Gran says, "We've sold the inn!"

When the words find my ears, everything goes fuzzy. Pops grabs my arm and steers me to a chair. "I told you it'd be a shock, Mabel."

Gran pats me on the shoulder. "I'm sorry, honey. I thought you'd be happy to have more free time."

Just what I'd been wishing for an hour ago. But not like this.

"Wh-where will you live?"

"We've been on a list at a retirement community down in Brunswick County for a while." Looking sheepish, my grand-mother says, "It did happen fast, but really, the timing was perfect. We put an ad in a couple of newspapers up north and got a bite just when a place opened up in the Villages."

"Isn't that all the way down by Oak Island? That's really far away!" I know I sound like a whiny little kid, but at the moment, I'm calling it a win that I'm not rolling on the floor in a tantrum.

"It's just forty minutes," Pops says.

"But I'm used to seeing you every day."

"Sweetheart, I know it's a big change," my grandmother says, stepping closer to Pops. "I'm sorry it's upsetting. I guess we thought we were cramping your style. Now that you've got a young man and your own business to run…"

She's right. I should be relieved. But instead, my head drops onto my arms, and I start to sob. "I don't want to leave. I'll miss you, and—I'll miss… everything."

Both of my grandparents make what are probably very reasonable arguments in soothing tones, but all I can do is cry.

This kitchen table holds every memory from my child-hood. I can practically taste every meal I've eaten here. My fingernails catch on the scratches I carved when I thought-lessly used an X-ACTO knife to cut up foam core for a class project. I got grounded for a week for marring the table, but now it's just a part of its character.

Eventually, though, I sit up. Disoriented, I accept the tissue Gran hands me, and I manage to blow my nose. But I'm too tired to talk to them. Maybe also too angry. Instead, I stumble up to my apartment and crawl into my bed and cry myself to sleep.

CHAPTER 15

Lawson's Reach, "Double Date"

Lawson discovers something about his feelings for Jill.

VIOLET

The next morning, banging on my door wakes me from a sleep so deep it takes me several moments to figure out where I am. But once I do, it only takes three seconds for me to figure out that I'm late to check in extras. Extremely late.

"Shit! Fuck!" I growl as I struggle to get untangled from sheets damp with sweat. "Goddammit! Ugh!"

"Vi? Hello?" Dani's voice calls from the other side of the door. "Are you okay?"

"Yes!" I yell back, before amending, "No! I mean, I'm alive, but I'm late and—" I begin to tear off the clothes I wore yesterday, also damp with sweat. What the fuck is wrong with me? And then it all comes back. My grandparents telling me they're selling the inn. Me freaking out.

"Violet! Let me in!"

"Hang on. I'm… naked."

I feel sick. Like I have a hangover. Not from alcohol but from crying. I never cry. The last time I cried was when I broke my arm in seventh grade. And that was from pain, not… feeling. It's one of the reasons I knew I'd never be an actress. I don't like those kinds of feelings.

Dani bangs on the door again.

"Okay, okay," I call, grabbing my robe and putting it on.

When I open the door, she walks straight to the kitchen and plunks down a bag of Britt's donuts and two to-go coffees. Skye's right behind her, and the dog makes a beeline for me. I sink to the ground to give her a hug, but before I can tell Dani that I have to get dressed and go because I completely fucked up and missed checking in background actors two hours ago, she holds up a hand.

"Your grandparents called me last night. They said you got really upset after they told you they're selling the inn. Which is totally understandable, by the way. I called Nate, and he went back to the office and picked up your call sheet and all the forms. Because you're anal as fuck, everything was there, so he knew where to go and what time to be there. He checked everyone in. All is well."

Tears threaten again, which pisses me off for some reason.

Dani just hands me a coffee and opens the bag of donuts. Instead of taking a single donut, I take the whole bag and wander over to the couch.

"You're welcome," she says, following me.

"Thank you," I mumble back with a mouth full of donut. Then I groan as the sugar hits. "You are a goddess."

"Glad we're clear on that." She takes the lid off her own cup of coffee, takes a donut from the bag, and dunks it.

Several minutes of mainlining caffeine and sugar later, she nudges my leg with her foot. "So, what happened?"

I shake my head, still in a daze. "I'm not really sure."

"You were upset because your grandparents are selling."

She makes it a statement, but one where there's a blank that needs to be filled at the end of it.

"Well, yeah. I grew up in that inn. I've never really lived anywhere else."

"You lived in a dorm the first year of college."

"Barely. I came back here every chance I got."

"Are you worried about them?"

"No. They seem really excited." A rush of feeling hits, and I grab another donut and stuff half of it in my mouth.

"So that's why you're upset."

I shrug.

"They're abandoning you the same way your parents did."

I roll my eyes even as I swallow a sob. "Thank you, Psych 101."

"It is pretty obvious."

"So, so what? So what if I'm sad and angry?"

"Nothing."

"Then why are you here?"

"Well, you're often angry, but you're never sad. I think Gran and Pops were a little unnerved. As am I, frankly."

Remembering how I'd stumbled out of their kitchen without even saying anything, I guess I can't blame them. And it might be true. Between Ford and Sully leaving town, the fact that the guy I'm getting attached to has an expiration date on him, and my grandparents selling my childhood home, I might have reached my abandonment limit for the week.

But nothing keeps me down for long.

I stuff the rest of donut number I'm-Not-Sure into my mouth and then grab a napkin. After washing the sugary dough down with a sweet, creamy gulp of coffee, I flick the icing crumbles off of my chest and wipe my mouth.

"Yeah, well, I'm fine now." I flash a big smile at Dani. "See?"

She sighs. "Right."

"But thanks for saving my ass this morning." When I stand up and more sugary bits fall on the floor, the dog's there to snuffle them up. "I've still got to go teach a class. I guess Skye can come with me."

"I can keep her for the day." Dani follows me back to the kitchen. "But are you sure you don't want to just take the day off?"

"Nope. I'm good. Thanks again for the treats."

She nods, drops her trash in the can and heads for the door. "Catch you later."

Before I make it all the way to the bathroom she calls, "Hey. When you have to move out of here, do you want to move in with me?"

I freeze in my tracks. I hadn't even really thought about the fact that I'd have to move too.

"I could use a roommate now that Whitney's moved out," she adds.

After turning around to study her expression, I say, "I thought you wanted some space."

"I did need a little time to myself." Sticking her hands in the back pockets of her cutoffs, she shrugs. "But if I don't get a roommate of my choice soon, my family will sniff out the fact that I've got a vacancy and one or two or five of my relatives will fill the void."

"Well," I say, more relieved and grateful than I'll ever admit. "I guess I could help you avoid that."

"Good," she says as she opens the door. "Then we won't have to drive the damn dog back and forth all the time. She can just stay in one place."

"Yeah. That'll be good," I agree. "See you later."

"See ya."

"Thanks again, Dan. For all of it."

"Anytime," she says.

NATE

Sunday morning, I head to the beach. Not to surf, but to do a cleanup. It's something I did on the regular with the Surfrider Foundation back in California, and something that's much needed here.

When Dani called to ask if I could check in extras yesterday, she told me the news Violet's grandparents had dropped. Violet herself dodged my calls Saturday, so I figured she needs some time to process the change.

It also feels good to be giving back with the community that has embraced me here. Maybe it's because we spend so much time in the water and on the sand, but surfers everywhere are pretty good about cleaning up not only after themselves but after those who thoughtlessly drop their cigarette butts, empty cans, and other trash on the beach.

Today I've got my eye out for something else too.

Ever since Dani gave me that piece of sea glass, I've been hoping to find others. They probably roll up on California beaches too, but I'd never noticed them before. There's something about the journey they take to get from trash to treasure that has stuck with me.

I'm about to pack up for the day when a pale red heart in the sand catches my eye. As I study it in the morning light, I can't quite believe my luck, but I know exactly what I'm going to do with it.

When Violet walks into my office Monday morning, she looks terrible. Her eyes are puffy and red, her hair is only partly up in a crazy bun, and her outfit is… odd. She's usually so put together. Not that she wears the kind of power suits my sister favors. Instead, she tends toward colorful sundresses cinched by belts that highlight her curves, with matching shoes and jewelry to complete the look. Not so beachy that she looks like she's on vacation, but appropriate for the hot, humid weather.

Today, her dress is sack-like, and her feet are in sneakers that look like she gardened in them recently. Her face is free of makeup, and she isn't sporting a single accessory.

We talked on the phone Sunday night, and she said she was fine. However, everything about her appearance this morning tells a different story: that her heart is broken and she's doing her best to keep her shit together. I get up and give her a gentle hug.

And then I have an idea.

"Can you do me a huge favor?" I whisper into her ear.

She leans back and attempts somewhat unsuccessfully to lift an eyebrow.

"Not that kind of favor."

She pouts.

"Unless you want that kind of favor. If you do…" I pointedly scan my office and its window that opens to the front room. "I'll do the best I can."

She just… wilts. I've never seen Violet without perfect posture. I've never seen her walk into a room without filling it with her presence. But right now, she's obviously operating on a very low battery.

"I hate to ask you this when you've probably got so much to do." The theatrical wince I add will definitely keep me from ever being cast in anything. "I've got an audition to run this afternoon, and my sister said that it's really important that we impress this director. Would you—could you—run the session for me?"

Her eyes light up instantly, but then she narrows them in suspicion. "This isn't because you feel sorry for me, is it?"

"Feel sorry for you?" Again, I do my best to inject my tone

with innocence, but I'm positive the performance falls flat when she adds lip pursing to the narrowing eyes. "I mean, I'll admit that I do want you to have a better day, but this is all about me saving my butt. My sister told me flat out that I'd better not fuck this up."

She nods slowly. "I would be happy to save you from your sister. And if it'll make *you* feel any better, I would like you to install the extra phone line and that fancy answering machine that we can program with lots of outgoing messages. I'm done with working late every damn night."

"Great," I say, doing my best not to get too excited at the prospect. "But we can schedule a meeting to go over that. If you want. Or I'll just do it."

"Just do it." She holds out a hand. "Can I have the sides and the schedule?"

I grab both and hand them to her.

She examines the autofill forms I created. "Wow, this is fancy."

I shrug, even though I'm pretty proud of them. "I made a template on the computer that makes it really easy. If someone has to cancel or reschedule, we can just plug in the new time or copy and paste their name and then print out the new version."

She holds the paper up to the light. "No Liquid Paper globs or anything."

"I also included this section where you can write your notes or check off these variables. Later, Betty will enter those in the computer so we can access them in the future."

"Huh," she says with interest.

When her focus shifts to the sides, I check my watch. "We have about fifteen minutes before the first appointment."

"Good thing I showed up, then," she says. "You want to run the camera?"

"Just like the old days with my dad." The few acting skills

I possess are no match for my all-too-real lack of enthusiasm about those old days.

"You don't have to."

"No, I want to. I mean, to be honest, I'd prefer to go out and pick up a new answering machine, but I think it'll be educational. For me," I add.

We move into the back room where I've got blackout curtains and lights set up, as well as a video recorder.

She looks around. "Nice setup."

"I just replicated what we've got back in LA." I check the camera to make sure we've got a fresh cassette. "Do you think you'll have them do any blocking for this?"

Looking over the script again, she shakes her head. "We'll have them slate standing but sit for the scene."

"Shall I have Betty send the first person in?" I ask.

"I'll get her." She pauses halfway through the doorway. "When I say we're just doing a rehearsal, make sure to tape it anyway. But don't let them know you're doing it. It's usually their best work."

The next hour is a revelation. When I heard that actors were disappointed with how I was running sessions, I thought it was because they expected some sort of coaching from me. Which I thought was ridiculous. I mean, isn't it their job to know how to act?

But what Violet does when an actor walks into the room is the in-person version of what she does with extras on the phone. If she knows them, she asks about some specific aspect of their lives or reminds them of a shared experience. She gets them to laugh, often at her own expense. By the time they step into the camera's frame, they're completely at ease. As planned, she tells them that we're just rehearsing, but I surreptitiously get the camera rolling.

When Violet reads the scene with the actor, she doesn't exactly perform, but she's not doing it in a monotone either.

She finds some in-between mode that somehow puts all the focus on the actor, while still giving them something to play off of.

After the first read, she asks them some sort of question about the character—not giving them direction, but planting a seed in their mind. Something else to focus on. After they've done it a couple of times and slated by saying their name and turning side to side to show profiles, she gives them a hug, tells them they did great, and walks them out the door.

Even when she doesn't know the actor, by the end of the audition, they're fast friends.

At the end of every casting session I've run in this office, I am completely wrung out. Something about the whole thing just puts me on edge, which I imagine may be rubbing off on the actors.

By the time we finish the last appointment of the afternoon, I'm not only convinced that I could never do what she does, I'm not sure my dad could either.

All I can say as I power down the camera is, "Well, that was different."

Her face falls, and I scramble to explain. "In a good way. In the best way. My dad runs these things like the actors are gladiators fighting to the death and he's the emperor with power over their fate. But you… it's like you want them to succeed. In here and in life."

"Because I do." She smiles—her full-on, one-hundred-watt smile—and I realize that I did indeed accomplish more today than creating better tape to send back to the director in LA. (My sister didn't read me the riot act. I kind of made that part up. But she will definitely be happier with these results.)

Most important, Violet has obviously completely forgotten her grief. At least for a little while.

VIOLET

By the end of the workday, I'm no longer pretending to be okay. Running the audition was a blast. As I'd hoped when I decided to make the leap to opening my own casting office, it was as fun as directing community theater actors, while getting paid good money to do it.

Even though things aren't yet where I want them to be, today gave me hope that Nate and I might be able to get them there. Not only was he truly relieved to let me run the audition, he obviously has skills and talents that I lack.

He's an old pro with the camera and took over the video edit and transfer for the audition tape so it can be FedExed to LA—a job I find tedious but one that he claims to enjoy. He's inordinately excited about setting up the new answering machine.

Man. I wonder if he likes bookkeeping? Now that would be sexy.

At the end of the day, I end up leaving the office before he does for the first time ever. I'm not only exhausted, but I need to have a calmer conversation with my grandparents, so I left him to it. After asking him to come over later.

My heart's still tender when I walk into the inn and think about all the memories that will have nowhere to live once she's in another owner's hands. Still, I don't want my grandparents to worry about me. They deserve to slow down. Plus, they're not my parents. At some point, they need to retire from that job too.

I take a deep breath before walking into the kitchen. It's the heart of the house, and it'll be the hardest to let go of, but no one needs an encore performance from me. When I push through the swinging doors, however, my grief is replaced by surprise. The room is full of loud, excited people. And dogs. Some of whom I recognize.

"Ben? Lucy? What are y'all doing here?"

Ben Porter is an actor who fell in love with Wallington when he did a movie here years ago. The summer after that, a friend of his got married at the Rumrunner. A memorable night for so many reasons. Since then, he's worked on a few projects down here, including *Lawson's Reach*, where it looks like he might've scored a recurring role as a high school teacher.

His wife Lucy often travels with him. She's like the big sister I wish I had and has shared her wealth of knowledge about training dogs with us since the moment we got Skye. But since Ben lit out of town after the hurricane with the group in Ford's car, I was afraid we'd never see him again.

"Meet the inn's new owners!" Pops cries.

"What? Ben and Lucy are buying it?"

"Not Lucy and me," Ben says as he puts his arm around an older man. "Violet, meet John Porter and Vera Rosen, my dad and stepmom. They're buying the inn. We're just along for the ride."

We shake hands as the couple explains that running an inn together will be a dream come true.

"Not to mention the chance to leave Boston winters behind," Mrs. Rosen adds. "I've had enough of them for a lifetime."

"Ben's experience with Hurricane Beverly didn't put you off?" I ask.

"We've lived through nor'easters and blizzards as well as a hurricane or two." Mr. Porter looks appreciatively around the kitchen. "And this old lady is obviously built to last. I'm looking forward to making sure she does so."

"My dad's a finish carpenter, but he knows pretty much everything about the building trades," Ben says with obvious pride.

After we spend a few more minutes catching up, Lucy and

Ben take the dogs out back. I follow my grandparents and the new owners-to-be into the front room, where we find George and Tina. The TV writers returned a few days ago to work on writing the hurricane episode.

"Back to the scene of the crime, as it were," Tina had said, a telltale blush coloring her cheeks. When they checked in, they were very concerned that they'd be back in "their room." The one I'd discovered them making out in when I went to tell them about the tornado warning, even though they hadn't seemed happy to have to share the room in the first place.

Now, they hop up from the couch the moment we enter the room.

"We heard you're the new owners," Tina begins.

"And we just want to say how glad we are that you plan to continue to operate it as an inn," George continues.

Tina bounces on her toes. "The thing is—"

George takes her hand. "We've developed kind of an attachment to our room."

Tina looks at George like he's got woodland creatures at his feet and birds circling his head. "And we'd really appreciate it if we could, basically, get first dibs on it when we come to stay."

As the bargaining continues, Gran takes me out into the hall. "I kind of thought that was coming," she whispers.

"They are a trip."

"You can say that again." She hooks her arm into mine, and we walk back to the kitchen. "Are you feeling better about things today, sweetheart?"

"I'm so sorry I lost it, Gran. That was totally uncalled for."

"I'm sorry it was such a shock." She pats my arm. "We should've prepared you for the news. But since you know the new owners, I'm sure you'll be able to visit anytime you like. They may even be willing to let you stay in the apartment."

I nod, still too full of feelings to get into all that. "We'll figure it out, I'm sure. I know you guys are ready to move on, and I promise I will be too. It'll just take me a little time."

"You take all the time you need. No one's rushing you. And you'll have a bedroom at our new place so you can visit anytime." Taking both my hands, she tugs on them until I meet her gaze. "Which you'd better do, you hear?"

"Yes, ma'am. You bet I will."

NATE

When we enter the theater Wednesday night, I have to admit that, once again, Violet was right. Nothing I'm seeing is anything like any premiere or cast and crew screening I ever attended in Hollywood.

There's one guy wandering around with a camera, but he's not harassing anyone, he's just there to cover the event for the local paper. There's a red carpet and a step-and-repeat, but everyone treats both like they're a joke. Best of all, I'm not the only one in shorts. I went with Bermudas and a polo shirt so as to not totally embarrass my date, who's in a dress and heels. But Vi's the one in the minority here. Most people have on the kind of company T-shirts and ball caps that shows give out on wrap day. The sheer variety of logos is a testament to the amount of work that gets done here.

And that seems to be the real focus. These are hard-working people that, like Violet, love what they do. They might be here to network, to hear about the next job coming down the line, but it feels different than the jockeying for power and cutthroat competition that ran in the background of every damn industry event I attended with my father.

Tonight feels like a community gathering to celebrate something they created together. A community I'm more and more convinced I'd like to be a part of. Thing is, the only way I can figure out how to join it is to leave it first.

VIOLET

As I drive Nate to the airport on Thursday afternoon, a knot of nerves gathers behind my solar plexus. Things are really good between us. Both at work and in the hours left outside of work, which, thanks to him, are getting longer.

But it feels almost too good to be true, too much like a rom-com movie with our meet-cute at the bar and the chemistry between us that has us bickering and banging in equal measure and with equal levels of passion. Like *When Harry Met Sally* crossed with *Jerry Maguire*. That is, if both Nate and I were sports agents instead of casting directors.

But now, not only is he leaving town, he's talking about quitting. Not me, but the business. He thinks he can talk his dad into closing the Fowler Stern satellite office here, but I think that's a long shot. And I'm not sure it's the best strategy.

Meanwhile, my grandparents are busy with moving plans, and I can't bury myself in work because Nate's done such a good job of streamlining everything. His sister made sure his schedule was clear for the week so he'd have no excuse to skip the trip home, so I can't even cover for him.

"Do you have plans for tonight?" he asks, breaking into my thoughts.

"I guess I'll see if Dani wants to take the dog to the beach." Taking a picnic to the beach at the end of the day, when all the tired and burned-to-a-crisp tourists are trudging away from the beach, used to be a regular thing for me and my friends. "There's nothing quite like relaxing in a beach

189

chair with a good basket of snacks and beverages as the sun goes down."

"Meanwhile, I'll be dealing with jet lag and family drama."

"I'll miss you."

He rests a hand on my thigh. "I'll miss you too."

"You're coming back, though, right?"

"Of course I am. You can't get rid of me that easy."

"Seriously, though. Don't push your dad too far. I know you think that I'm losing out on my dream, but it doesn't really matter who's in charge."

When he doesn't say anything in return, I glance over at him. "I mean it. I'm making enough money, and now that the local manager finally let me run the casting sessions, I'm happy."

He puffs out a laugh and squeezes my thigh. "I'm happier about that than you are, believe me, but I also don't like that we're lying to my dad. He doesn't know that you're doing the background casting. He still wants me to run you out of business."

"Well, having him throw a hissy fit and kick us both to the curb when you tell him would be worse."

We arrive at the airport, and for once I wish the ride were longer. After I park in front of the terminal, he leans over to kiss my cheek. When I don't turn to kiss him back, he says, "Hey. I know we still have a lot to work out at the office, but I'm not going anywhere. I mean, I am today, but… you know what I mean, right?"

I don't want him to leave with things awkward between us, so I hop out of the car. "You sure you don't want me to come in and wait?"

He looks at his watch. "It's okay. Boarding's in like ten minutes, so by the time you park, I'll be on the plane."

He grabs his carry-on from the back seat, throws it over his shoulder, and then pulls me into a hug. "It'll be late by the time I get in tonight, but I'll call you at the office tomorrow, okay?"

"Okay." I give him a squeeze and a quick kiss. "Don't miss your flight."

Then he gives me one last kiss and heads into the terminal, while my gut tells me things are about to change.

Again.

CHAPTER 16

LAWSON'S REACH, "ROAD TRIP"

LAWSON ENDS UP ON A ROAD TRIP WHILE CHARLI FACES NEW PROBLEMS.

NATE

THE MINUTE WE LAND IN LA AND I TURN ON MY CELL PHONE, IT rings. After two long flights, all I want is to fall into bed. But my sister has other ideas.

"The kids want to see you, so we're coming to pick you up," Monica says without preamble.

Since she booked my flight, I guess it makes sense that she knows my schedule. "It's been a long day, Monica. I'm on east coast time."

"Do you want to deny your niece and nephew time with their favorite uncle?"

"You mean their only uncle?"

"Details, details."

"All right. I didn't check a bag, and we're about to deplane."

"We're in a white minivan. See you in a few."

She hangs up before I can give her shit about buying a

minivan. Five minutes later I'm crawling past my niece and nephew, both strapped into booster seats, to collapse in the back row of the van. "Nice ride, sis."

She turns around and sticks her tongue out at me. "Shut up, asshole."

"That's a quarter, Mommy," my niece Brittany says primly.

My brother-in-law catches my eye in the rearview mirror. "You always bring out the best in her, Nate."

"It's a gift," I say over a yawn.

"We're going to In-N-Out for dinner, Uncle Nate," Joshua practically shouts. He always gets loud when he's excited.

"Awesome," I say offering up a hand for a high five. "I could go for an Animal Style burger and a shake."

"Me too," Brittany says.

My sister groans. She normally only allows them healthy stuff, but I guess she's trying to make getting Uncle Nate from the airport an event. Her attention is quickly redirected to giving her husband directions to avoid traffic.

"Adam, what are you doing? We're not taking the 405. You want to cut through Westchester and Marina Del Rey to get to the one in Venice. By the Costco?"

Instead of blowing up at her, he calmly replies, "Right. Sorry. I was just on autopilot."

The last time I hung out with my sister and her family, there'd been a lot of tension between her and Adam. But by the time we're stuffed into a booth at my favorite LA takeout place stuffing our faces with food, the two of them are giggling. He gives her shit about ordering a Protein Style burger, and she claims she only wanted a couple fries. Before eating half of his.

It's a hell of a lot more fun than the passive-aggressive sniping they usually engage in, but it does make me wonder what's going on.

Meanwhile, my niece and nephew have me laughing with

their one-upmanship, each trying to tell me a better story about what's going on in their lives. I'm too tired to absorb it all, but I do manage to nod and ask appropriate questions as they fill me in on the latest with their pets and friends and school.

They beg me to have a sleepover, but that's where I put my foot down. It may be nine o'clock here, but my body thinks it's midnight.

"Uncle Nate needs to get his beauty sleep, and that won't happen in your bunk bed," my sister explains to Joshua. "But we'll see him all day tomorrow."

"You will?" I ask.

"Didn't you get my message?"

"If you left it on my cell, then no. Coverage in Wallington is spotty, so I've stopped checking it."

"We all took the day off to spend it with you," she says.

"You took a day off?" My sister is as much of a workaholic as my dad. "Wait, is something wrong?"

Adam puts his arm around her. "We're just trying some new strategies."

It's clear that he doesn't want to get into their marriage issues in front of the kids, so I just nod. I was hoping to get in some time on the water tomorrow, but if my sister's making the effort to act like a family, I guess I can too.

As we pile back into the car and they drive me to my apartment in Mar Vista—a temporary place I sublet the last time I came home—the kids tell me all about our plans for the next day: the Long Beach aquarium in the morning and the Santa Monica pier in the afternoon, followed by dinner with Grandpa.

At least two of the three items on the agenda will be fun.

One of the few things my sister and I have in common is that we are terrified of rollercoasters. Even the kiddie-sized ones. She seems to have married one fan and spawned two, however, so we get in line for ice cream while Adam takes the kids on the ride.

Since our time alone is limited, I jump right in to ask some sisterly advice. We may be opposites in almost every way, but that doesn't keep me from looking up to her. "Got any advice for your little brother about relationships?"

She gives me a long look before answering. "When I told you to make nice with the girl who does background casting in Wallington, I didn't mean *that* nice."

No surprise that my sharp-as-a-tack sister has figured me out. "I'm not even going to ask how you know."

"It's how you say her name, dumbass. 'Violet this' and 'Vi that' like she invented water. You're so transparent."

"I don't know why I'm asking the woman who almost filed for a divorce a year ago for advice, but I am."

"What's the problem?"

"I'm afraid that we want different things."

Before she can answer, I hold up a hand. "No, that's not it. I'm not sure what she wants from me."

She opens her mouth, but I stop her again. "Honestly? I'm afraid she's too much like Dad."

Monica just raises her eyebrows in response to that.

"In that work is everything to her."

"And you don't want to compete for her attention," she says with a nod.

"I think I've done enough of that for one lifetime."

"With Dad and work?"

"What else?"

"I don't know." She shrugs. "Me?"

"You think I'm in competition with you?"

"I think we all competed for Dad's limited attention. You, me, and Mom. Mom just bowed out early."

This is news to me. I always thought Monica and my dad were totally simpatico. "I never felt like I was even on Dad's radar. Like his priorities were work and the ego strokes he got from success at work, then you, then people he works with, then me."

She shakes her head definitively. "You're wrong about that. You're very important to him."

"He has a very strange way of showing it."

"He does. I think it's how he was raised. To push the people you love most the hardest."

I blow out a breath. "I did not intend this to be a talk about me and Dad."

"I hate to tell you, honey, but you can't bring your whole self to a relationship until you've figured out your shit with your family."

"Then Vi and I are doomed. Her parents left her with her grandparents while they went to work anywhere in the world but where she is. Our parents may have been in town, but they basically ignored us."

Her face softens, and she bumps shoulders with me. "I get it, but everybody has some kind of family issues to deal with. And patterns they developed to cope. For you, it's running away."

"Yeah, well, for you, it's pretending that it's not happening."

"You think I don't know that?" She shakes her head. "It did take me some time to figure out that I *can* make other choices. I mean, Mom's a self-involved flake, and Dad's a narcissist. I can get along with them by ignoring that and focusing on their better qualities. But pretending Adam and I didn't have issues? It was either face them or give up."

Monica's focus flicks to something behind me briefly. "Adam and the kids are coming this way, so I'll make this short and sweet. I learned two things in therapy. One, see the other person for who they are, not who you want them to be.

Two, bend a little. Not so much that you break, but enough to make a difference."

"Okay, Dr. Drew."

"You'll thank me someday, I guarantee it."

She turns to greet her family and then pulls her husband in for a kiss. "Good timing. We're next in line."

Later that evening, after we've celebrated my dad and my sister and her family go home, I offer to do the dishes.

"I won't say no. It'll make the housekeeper happy," my dad says as he pours himself a scotch. He offers me the same, but I beg off since I have to drive back to my place and catch an early flight in the morning.

As I rinse the plates, I can see my dad's face reflected in the window over the sink. He looks older and a lot less intimidating than he does in my imagination. Eyes back on the job at hand, I decide to take the plunge.

"I have a favor to ask you," I begin.

"You meet a pretty actress in Carolina that needs a leg up in the business? No problem."

"Not exactly." I brace myself for whatever cutting remarks my request will elicit. "I want you to close Carolina Casting."

"Really? You're giving up after just a few weeks?"

I take my time closing the dishwasher and drying my hands, then I make myself face my father. "I'm not giving up. I want *you* to give up on the feud, and I want to work with Violet."

"Who's Violet?"

"The woman who turned you down. The woman you wanted me to destroy."

Before he can argue, I hold up my hand to stop him, even though it's shaking slightly. "Hear me out, please? Violet has been doing background casting in Wallington part-time for years. She also worked for Jay doing local casting. So when Uncle Rob picked up *Lawson's Reach*, she decided to open her own company, knowing that she'd have a steady stream of work."

"And when I cut that off…"

"It screwed her over."

"And now you're screwing her and want to make her happy. At my expense."

Pushing aside the fact that somehow my family can read me like a book, I push back. "There's enough work in Carolina for one casting company that does both day player and extras casting. But not two."

"I still don't see why it should be her. Why not us?"

"She's put in the time and done all the legwork already. She has the contacts and community trust to reliably populate any background needs."

"How do you know?"

I take a deep breath before answering. "Because I've been subbing that work out to her."

"Behind my back?"

"I'm sorry about that, but it was the smart thing to do." Deciding not to throw my sister under the bus, I add, "And Violet's damn good at running an audition. I asked her to do one for me this week after I overheard an actor complaining about how horrible I was to audition for."

"What does that mean? That you didn't hold his hand and tell him he was perfect?" The sneer returns to his face, and I'm ashamed to admit that I'm relieved it's aimed at someone else. It occurs to me that I may have been bringing a load of unresolved anger into the audition room with me, pent up from every Saturday I had to sit through similar sessions just to spend time with him, but now doesn't seem like the best time to get into that.

"All I can say is, compare Tuesday's tape to anything I sent in the past few weeks, and it'll be clear."

"If I were to do as you ask, where will that leave you? Will you come back and work for me?"

"No. I'm staying in North Carolina."

Before the words were out of my mouth, I hadn't been sure. But now that I've said them, it's clear. Of course, I'm going back. All that matters is that the woman I want to spend all my days with is there.

"So you're just leaving your family. Again." For once, the expression on his face isn't full of judgement. He just looks confused and maybe a little hurt, and I suddenly realize that I don't have to hate him. I'm never going to change him, but I can still care about him.

And that feels okay.

"I'll come home to visit, and you're welcome to visit me anytime. I've finally found a place that feels like home to me and a person that I want to make a home with." I meet his eyes and find the courage to let him see me. The real me. "I love her, Dad."

"What are you going to do there?"

"Whether you close the Wallington office or not, I'm going to work for Violet. And I'm going to start a chapter of the Surfrider Foundation in Wallington."

Two more things I didn't know I wanted until I said them aloud. I don't know how exactly I'll make it all work, but I'm determined to try.

Because it's true. I love her.

My dad finishes off his whiskey and then turns to face me. "Will you stay for the whole weekend instead of leaving tomorrow? So we can talk this through and make a plan?"

CHAPTER 17

LAWSON'S REACH, "DECISIONS"

LAWSON JOINS CHARLI WHEN SHE GOES TO VISIT HER FATHER.

VIOLET

EVEN THOUGH OUR SCHEDULE IS LIGHT WHILE NATE'S AWAY, there's always paperwork, so I go into the office Saturday morning to do a bit of catching up. I'm in the middle of filling out union forms when the phone rings. Nate and I spoke briefly last night before the dinner with his dad. I was glad to hear that he'd had a good day with his sister and her family, but I've been nervously awaiting any news about his dad and the business. He'd said he planned to talk to his dad after dinner, so it'd be too late to call me afterwards.

Thinking it might be him, I pick up just before the machine does. "This is Violet."

"Hey, Violet. It's Jay."

"Hello, stranger. What can I do you for?" Whatever happens with Nate and his dad, I'm not burning the bridge I've got with the east coast Fowlers.

"Well, I just heard a little gossip, and I thought I should give you a heads-up."

"Work coming my way soon?"

"Maybe. A little bird who works in the Wallington Studios offices called me this morning to let me know that Alan Fowler left a message late last night wanting to know what it'd cost to break his lease."

"Wow. You have ears everywhere."

"I do my best. But this gal owes me one, and she said she'd fill me in on anything having to do with that bastard. Anyway, sounds to me like he's thinking about closing the office in Wallington. Meaning my cousin will move on, and you'll have the town to yourself again."

"Nate's leaving." Suddenly I don't even have the energy to lift the last syllable of my sentence into a question.

"I mean, that was going to happen eventually. Nate's never been able to settle anywhere. Always finds something that he doesn't like about whatever he's doing and moves on. And as far as I could tell, he just took the job in Wallington to suck up to his dad. He hates working in casting."

When I don't say anything, Jay fills the silence. "So, congratulations."

Yeah, and for some stupid reason I don't feel like celebrating, echoes in my head as I mumble a goodbye to Jay and hang up the phone.

But then I remember Nate's words when I dropped him off at the airport less than forty-eight hours ago. *I'm not going anywhere.*

It's highly likely that Jay's opinions about Nate are colored by his father's antipathy for the entire west coast clan. Nate himself has admitted that he's had a hard time settling anywhere, but not only has he told me that he wants to be here, he's made connections with others in the community. We haven't made any specific plans about the future of the casting office, but as long as his dad doesn't take a hit out on me or something, I'm confident we can work that out. And I'm pretty sure that Nate wants to.

Still, I'd like to hear it from the horse's mouth. It's only when I pick up the phone to dial that I realize I only know his number at his apartment here in Wallington. He called yesterday, but I didn't think to get his cell. Thinking I can try information to see if he's listed in Los Angeles, I pick up the phone, but there's no dial tone. Instead, there's static. "Uh, hello?"

"Hello," a familiar voice answers.

"Mom?" Not only do my parents rarely call, but I didn't know they had this number. "What's wrong?"

"The phone didn't even ring!" she says after a telltale delay.

International calls are always filled with annoying pauses as well as static, so I know they must still be in Brazil. Unless they've moved on to someplace else.

"It didn't here either. I was about to make a call."

"Well, I'm glad we caught you. We tried the inn, and Mother gave me this number. We've got a surprise."

"Really?" Surprises from my parents make me nervous. Usually it's an odd gift—like a shrunken head or a prayer shawl blessed by a shaman—but once they sent what turned out to be a Schedule I narcotic.

"Yes! We've put enough miles in your frequent flier account for you to fly down and visit us. They were about to expire and we can't get away, so we gave them to you. You do have to use them this week, though."

"Oh. Well, thank you. But I can't leave this week."

"But don't you have the summer off from teaching?"

I swear that I've told my parents that I'm now doing casting full time, but since it had nothing to do with them, they likely forgot.

I used to get so upset when they'd forget things I told them. Or my birthday or my high school graduation. But right now I just feel sad for them. I'm a pretty cool person, and they don't even know me.

"Actually, I don't have the summer off." Another phone line starts blinking, saving me from having to explain again. "But again, thanks for the invite. I have to go, but say hi to Dad for me."

She insists on putting my dad on so I can do it myself and then he rambles on about something having to do with their current project. By the time I hang up, whoever was trying to get through on the other line has too. And there's no message on the machine. If it was Nate, he'll probably try my apartment next, so I decide to finish the paperwork later and head home.

Ten minutes later, I do indeed find a blinking light on my home machine, and I can't push the play button fast enough.

"Vi, it's me." Even over the tinny speaker, the man's voice makes my knees weak. "Listen, I hope this won't leave you in the lurch at the office, but I changed my flight. Things didn't go as expected with my dad. Call me, and I'll explain." He almost sounds like he's getting choked up, and there's a slight pause before he continues. "Actually, I really wish you could be here too because—"

But before he can finish, the recording breaks off and the answering machine makes an awful squealing sound. I press play again, but that has it making a grinding noise. And when I carefully open the window to the little cassette, it's clear that the machine has eaten the tape. With shaking hands I try to thread it back in, but no matter what I do, it won't play again.

"Goddammit!" I yell, throwing the machine on the floor. "Fuck! You wish I could be there because what? Are you not coming back? Is your dad dying? What?"

But then I realize I have a way to find out.

Thank you, Mom and Dad.

In less than two hours, I manage to book a ticket to Los Angeles with the miles my parents gave me, pack, make sure Dani can keep Skye, warn Mrs. Wilson that she'll be on her own at the office Monday, say goodbye to my grandparents, and make it to the airport in time for departure.

I feel like I could conquer anything. I'm free. Free of the burden of trying to make my parents love me. And buoyed by another truth.

I love Nate, and I'm pretty sure he loves me. I just have to make sure he knows that I want him to stay in Wallington, that whatever his dad is up to, we can make it work somehow. Even if I have to move to LA, it'll all be okay.

A few worries do creep in, though. What if this is a bad idea? What do I know about being in love, after all?

But then I think of my friends. Even if Dani's the only one who's left, they love me, and I love them. If push came to shove, we'd do anything for each other.

In fact, if I can't find Nate after I land, I'm hoping Ford will let me crash with him.

I spend the flight from Wallington to Charlotte buzzing from adrenaline. By the time the plane from Charlotte to LAX takes off, the emotional toll and lack of sleep over the past few weeks hits me hard. I tuck the pillow I pilfered from first class between my head and the window, and the next thing I know, the flight attendant is announcing that we're about to land.

Once my feet hit the ground in California, I'm full of purpose and energy again. I find a bank of pay phones and call Ford. He doesn't answer, so I leave him a message letting him know I'm in town and giving him my beeper number. My next call is Information. Unfortunately, there are a whole bunch of Nathaniel Fowlers in the LA area. The woman asks me if I want to narrow it down by neighborhood or area code, but I don't know the answer to either of those questions. I never asked where he lives in LA; I don't even know if he kept an apartment here. I thought he'd always be in the office right next door.

Before I hang up, however, I get the listing for Fowler Stern Casting, then I head to the taxi stand and give the driver the Beverly Hills address.

That's when my luck ends.

My flight landed at four-thirty. I figured I'd have plenty of time to get from the airport to the casting office before people head home for the day, even on a Saturday. But I quickly discover that driving around Los Angeles is nothing like driving around Wallington. We haven't even made it out of the airport by five o'clock, and the traffic is stop-and-go from then on out.

I lean forward to ask the taxi driver, "Um, how long do you think it'll take to get to my destination?"

He just points to the sea of red lights ahead of us.

"So, maybe, six o'clock?"

"Lady, you're gonna be lucky to get there to*day*."

I flop back into my seat and wonder if I should just have the guy take me to Ford's place.

Then I remember that Nate always complained about his father working long hours. Nate may not be there, but maybe I'll get lucky and his father will be there slaving away.

Every minute that passes, along with each tick upward on the meter, chips away at my confidence. By the time the taxi pulls up in front of the office building where Fowler Stern Casting is located and I hand over every bit of my cash to pay the fare, I'm about ready to cry uncle. I don't know what I was thinking. I don't know anything about this town and how things work. I'm just a washed-up high school drama teacher from a hick town nobody here has ever heard of.

It's now after 7:30 p.m., so I can only hope that Alan

Fowler really is a serious workaholic. Nate is probably out getting sushi or something with his fabulous LA friends. Who I know nothing about because I never asked.

Fate does smile on me, if somewhat dimly. After I push through the revolving door into the marbled lobby, the security guard just points at a sign-in sheet and tells me the workshop is on the fourth floor.

"The workshop?" I ask.

"Aren't you here for the acting workshop?"

"Oh, yes, sorry," I fib. "I just think of it as more of a… class. You know."

"Whatever you call it, everyone else got here an hour ago. You better hustle on up there."

"I will, thanks."

After I step out of the elevator, I follow the signs reading "Auditions 101 with Alan Fowler" and the sound of voices down the hall until I find a classroom with a camera pointed at an actor in a chair. Other students sit in a few rows of chairs facing him.

When I slip in the door, one person turns around, but her focus flicks back to the stage as soon as a man says, "Let's go again."

Seeking the source of the voice, my eyes land on a preview of Nate in thirty years. If Nate turned into the kind of guy who'd dye his hair shoe-polish black and get a spray-on tan, that is.

Alan Fowler runs the class just like I expected he would. He gives little direction to the actor in the hotspot and instead spends the next forty-five minutes barely listening to anyone but himself. In between reads, instead of giving feedback, he regales his audience with story after story of famous actors he's worked with. Few of the so-called students seem to mind, however. They lean toward him like flowers seeking the sun. Or like subjects hoping to catch the king's favor.

An hour later, my jaw is tight from keeping it closed. I

have plenty to say to these hopefuls about what they could do to improve their auditions. Because I *do* know what I'm doing. I may not be able to drop names like Alan Fowler, but if given the opportunity, I'd get camera-ready performances out of any of these people.

By the time he ends the class with a ridiculous bow of false humility, I'm rarin' to go. I can't watch the students fawn over him, so I wait just outside the classroom. When he finally exits, I step forward.

"Mr. Fowler, may I speak with you?"

His brow furrows. Or it looks like it's trying to, making me wonder if he's done that Botox thing I read about in *Allure* magazine. Apparently, it's all the rage here in La-La Land to pay a dermatologist to inject poison under your skin to get rid of wrinkles.

"If you didn't get a turn in class," Mr. Fowler says, "you'll have to come back next week. We went over time as it is."

"No, I'm not a student. I'm Violet Davenport."

His too-charming smile fades, and he gives me a calculating once-over. "So you're the woman my son wants me to give in to."

"I'm—" My impulse to fight for what I want from this man falters. "What do you mean 'give in to'?"

He crosses his arms over his chest and leans a shoulder against the wall behind him. "He wants me to close my office in Wallington."

It's my turn to narrow my eyes at him. "And are you going to do that?"

He waves a hand in the air. "I've made my point to my brother, and Nate's right. In the long run, it's much more efficient to contract with you than to pay someone to be there full time and support an entire office."

Before I can ask if everything else is okay, he straightens and looks pointedly at his watch.

"Was there anything else I could do for you, Ms. Davenport? I do still have calls to make."

I came here spoiling for a fight, and I didn't get one. He doesn't look like he's dying, unless the Botox gets him, so I decide to get in at least one punch before I go back to my corner in Wallington.

"Do you even know why he wanted to take on the job in North Carolina?"

He puffs out a cynical laugh. "To prove me wrong, I'm sure."

"Prove you wrong?"

"To prove that he could actually stay in one place for three months. I guess he was wrong about that."

"From where I sit, it looked like he wanted to prove that he belongs."

"That's ridiculous. Of course he belongs. He's my son."

"Maybe you'll want to have a look at your priorities, then, because he doesn't feel like he's one of them."

He presses his lips together briefly before thanking me for my insights and turning to walk down the hall. Just as he disappears into a doorway, I remember that I still need Nate's phone number, so I jog after him. "Excuse me, sir?"

He looks up from his desk. "What else can I do for you, Ms. Davenport?"

"I forgot that I meant to ask you for Nate's local phone number."

"Just call him on his cell."

"I don't have that number."

"I thought you two were close."

"We are. But, well, cell service in Wallington is terrible, so I never thought I'd need it. And I didn't tell him I was coming here, so I don't know how to find him."

He attempts a frown—unsuccessfully, cementing my guess that he's done Botox—before pulling out a message pad. As he writes, I take in the view behind him through the giant plate glass windows. I don't know my LA geography, but they are hills and they're lit up, so maybe they're the Hollywood Hills. I'm looking for the famous sign when he hands me a slip with two phone numbers on it.

"That's what I have for him."

"Okay. Thanks."

"Thank you again for sharing your perceptions, Violet."

The guy could never be an actor, but he'd be awfully good at poker. I have no idea of the subtext under his words because he's hidden his feelings as well as he's hidden his wrinkles and his gray hair.

I get off the elevator thinking that I should be ecstatic. Instead, I feel… deflated. And it's not just that I have nowhere to stay, no cash to pay a taxi, and no actionable plan.

Something's missing.

Thinking that it's just that I'm missing someone to share the good news with, I ask the doorman for directions to the pay phones and hope that I still have money on my calling card. I do have a couple quarters left, so I try Nate's local number first. There's no answer and the message is a generic one, so I'm not even sure that it's still his number. I leave a message anyway, telling him that I'm in LA for another twelve hours or so and that I'll try again later.

Then I try Ford, who, thankfully, does pick up.

"Hey, Ford. It's me, Vi."

"Hey, Vi. Everything okay?"

"Yeah, everything's fine. Listen, I'm sorry I haven't called since you left town, but guess what? I'm in LA."

"What? What are you doing here?

"Good question. But I've just used my last quarter, so I need to make this quick."

"Do you want to come over?"

"I thought you'd never ask."

He gives me his address, and then I say, "Here's the thing, I spent all my cash on the last taxi I took. I could try and get another one, but I'd have to borrow money from you to pay him."

"You'll never get a cab on the street. It's not like New York. You'd have to call for one. Where are you?"

I give him the address, and he takes a few minutes to look at a map. "I can come get you, but it'll be about half an hour."

"Are you su—?"

"Please deposit another twenty-five cents to continue your call."

"I'll be outside the front of the building, Ford. Thanks for doing this."

"No problem. I'll see yo—"

And we get cut off.

Now that I have a place to stay and a ride, I pull out my calling card. After punching the many digits of the card number and my pin and the automated voices prompts me to enter the number I'd like to call, I dial what I hope is still Nate's cell number. The line rings and rings. Just when I'm about to give up, it picks up.

"Hello?"

"Boy, am I glad to hear your voice."

"Violet? Where are you?"

"Well, as it turns out, I'm in LA."

"What? What are you doing here?" he asks, echoing Ford's words. Problem is, I still don't have an answer.

"You know, I'm not really sure. It all seemed so clear when I was trading airline miles for my ticket, but now I'm just confused."

"Okay?"

"When I got here, I realized I didn't have your phone number, so I went to Fowler Stern. I found your dad, and he told me he's closing your office, which, weeks ago would've made happy, but now it doesn't."

He doesn't say anything about what he's planning to do now or what he feels about me, which makes my mouth run faster. "Maybe you've rubbed off on me. Maybe I don't want to just work all the time anymore. Maybe running my own business and being self-sufficient isn't the most important thing in the world."

"What is the most important thing?"

"I… I think it's—"

"You have fifteen seconds left on this call," an automated voice cuts in.

"What? Fifteen seconds? I thought I was supposed to get a warning at one minute!"

"She can't hear you, you know," Nate says, laughing.

"This isn't funny. I need to talk to you."

But before I can even ask for his address, the only thing I'm talking to is dial tone.

By the time Ford picks me up I'm so happy to see a familiar face I could cry. But what I do instead is fall asleep. Ford manages to get me into his apartment and into bed without really waking me up, I guess, because when I wake, the clock on his bedside table says that it's 5:00 a.m.

I try to roll over and go back to sleep, but it's no use. I'm still on east coast time. Even though Nate probably is too, I don't want to risk waking whoever he's staying with. An image of some gorgeous, model-thin California blonde pops into my head, but I swat it away. I may not be sure if Nate is in love with me as much as I am with him, but I do trust that he wouldn't cheat on me.

What I don't know is: Will he want to leave his family for me? Mr. Stern made it sound like Nate wasn't planning to stay in Wallington, and when Nate called Friday afternoon, he seemed so jazzed after spending the day with his sister and her family. He has a niece and nephew here, and I'm pretty sure he's their only uncle. Whereas I'm an only child. My grandparents and Dani are the only family I have left.

Except for the giant extended family that is the Wallington film community.

Is it fair to ask Nate to leave his blood relatives behind for that?

I haven't been here twenty-four hours, and I know I'd never last in LA. It's too big, too flashy, too everything.

I know I'm spinning, so I decide to take a shower, get ready as quietly as possible, and then try and call Nate. Sneaking out of Ford's room, I find my bag in the living room and take it into the bathroom with me. Once I'm showered and in clean clothes, I repack everything and then get coffee going. Once that's ready, I call Nate's cell.

"Where are you?" he asks as soon as he hears my voice.

"I'm at Ford's apartment," I whisper.

"Why are you whispering?" he whispers back.

"Because it's 6:00 a.m. and Ford is still sleeping." It feels weird to talk to him when I can't picture where he is. "Where are you?"

"In my apartment."

"In Wallington?"

"No, no. In Mar Vista."

"Where's that?"

"It's a neighborhood. Actually, I think it used to be a city in its own right, but it got swallowed up at some point."

"By what?"

"Los Angeles."

"Oh. Okay. I'm a little confused here."

"Should I come get you?"

"Do you want to?"

"Yes, Violet. I want to tell you what happened when I

talked to my dad, and I really want to know what made you jump on a plane to come out here."

"Um, okay. I just have to figure out where I am exactly." I take Ford's cordless phone out the front door of his apartment, which opens onto a courtyard. "I can see the street from here, but I don't know its name."

"Go look. I'll wait."

"Okay." Setting the phone on a table by the door, I go out into the surprisingly cool morning. I have to walk all the way to the corner to get the name of Ford's street, so I'm breathing heavily by the time I get back.

"It's called Mammoth Avenue. 4325 Mammoth Avenue."

"In…?"

"Los Angeles? Isn't that where we are?"

"Yes, but the city is divided into hundreds of neighborhoods. Smaller cities, too. But don't worry, I'll look it up in the *Thomas Guide*."

"What are you doing?" Ford asks from behind me.

"Jesus!" I squeal.

"Everything okay?" Nate asks in my ear.

"Yeah, except that Ford just about gave me a heart attack."

"You're the one up at the ass crack of dawn going in and out of my house," Ford says over a yawn.

"Sorry, I was just trying to figure out where we are so Nate could come and get me."

Ford sighs. "Give me the phone."

Scowling, I hand it over. He says hello to Nate, gives him directions, and then hangs up.

"Hey! I didn't get to say goodbye."

"Do I smell coffee?"

I smack him, but then I hustle to the kitchen and pour him a cup of coffee. He sits at the bar in the kitchen. "Make yourself at home, why dontcha?"

I glare at him and stop mid-pour. "Do you want coffee or not?"

He just makes a gimme gesture.

When I don't comply, he wilts. "Come on, Vi. You got me up before the birds. I need some coffee."

After taking a few sips of the coffee I hand over, he says, "He's about a half hour away, so you've got time to tell me what the hell is going on. Starting with why you're here. Did you try some grand romantic gesture to win Nate back that failed or something?"

"Get Nate back?" My heart practically stops. "Do you know something I don't? Have you been talking to Sully about us?"

"Uh, not exactly. One, I'm still mad at him, and two, he's out in the middle of some ocean, isn't he?"

I rub my forehead. "Yeah, right. I'm just a little confused, I guess."

"So why did you come to LA?"

I take a fortifying gulp of my own cup of coffee, hoping the caffeine will make things clearer. "I came to tell Nate I want him to stay in Wallington, but what I learned was that Mr. Fowler decided to close up shop."

"Isn't that what you wanted?"

"That's the thing. It doesn't feel like it. I should be over the moon, but I'm just…"

"Just what?"

"Feeling feelings I don't understand."

"Like?"

"Instead of feeling, like, triumphant that I won, I'm more worried about what Nate's going to do now. Instead of feeling happy that I can be totally in charge again, I feel… bereft."

He pats me on the knee. "Sounds like you need to have a talk with Nate."

"I just hope things turn out the way I want them to."

"And what's that?"

"I want him to come back to Wallington. I want you to

come back too, and Sully. And I want Whitney to answer my calls." I shrug. "I know you think I'm living in a fairy tale, but… you asked."

He puts down his coffee cup and takes my hand. "I'm sorry about what I said that night, Vi. After the hurricane and everything. I didn't really mean it."

I look down into my coffee. "You were probably right."

He tugs on my hand until I meet his gaze. "I wasn't. I was just… being an idiot."

"Are you coming back?"

He looks around his apartment, which looks barely lived in. There's nothing on the walls, and he's got the bare minimum of furniture. But before he can answer, the doorbell rings.

CHAPTER 18

Lawson's Reach, "Decisions"

Lawson reveals his true feelings for Charli.

NATE

When Ford's apartment door opens and I see Violet's weary but still gorgeous face, my smile's so big it hurts.

Until I watch her expression go from surprise, to confusion, to anger. Stunned, I stand stock still while she proceeds to pummel my chest with her fists. Thankfully, her upper body strength is nil, so it doesn't hurt.

"Hi?" I attempt in greeting.

"I. Am. So. Mad. At. You." She pants between punches before giving up, dropping her hands, and thunking her forehead into my sternum.

"Ow," we say in unison. She straightens, rubbing her head and my chest as if she needs to make it feel better.

Ford sticks his head out from a doorway. "Hiya, Nate. I'm just going to… go in the other room."

After a door closes, I turn back to Violet. "What did I do now?"

"I thought you'd abandoned me."

"I told you I was going to LA for my dad's birthday."

"But then you talked him into closing the office. Now you have nowhere to work."

"I just made it clear that he was wasting money trying to compete with you and that no one can do what you're doing." Her gaze shifts towards the windows, and it looks like there might be tears in her eyes. "Is that not what you wanted?"

"Of course it's what I wanted!" she yells.

"But you don't want that anymore?"

"No!" The fists are back, but they're clutched at her sides rather than hitting me.

"What *do* you want?"

"You, you dummy!"

"Okay."

"Okay, what?"

"Okay, you can have me."

"But you don't have family in Wallington. Or a job. You'll have to go to Ohio or Idaho or wherever it is that you're always wandering off to."

"I'm sorry, but I'm really not sure what you're talking about."

A finger pokes me in the chest. "You said it yourself! When you first got to Wallington, and then you told Dani, and then Jay said it too."

"Said what?"

"That you only last for a short time."

"I think you of all people would have to disagree with that."

She groans. "I don't mean in bed. I mean at a job, in a place, in a relationship."

"Yeah, well, that was before a gorgeous woman threw herself at me—"

"Pfft." She rolls her eyes. "Like that's never happened

before, Mr. Dylan-slash-Dermot lookalike."

I'm still struggling to keep up with wherever her brain is spinning to. "I'm going to back up. When I agreed to take the job in Wallington, I figured I'd go there and kick ass for a couple months—proving to my dad that I'm not a total fuck-up—and then come back to be welcomed like the prodigal son. But instead of killing a fatted calf, my dad would listen to me and stop working eighty-hour weeks."

"Because you hate that he's a workaholic."

"Right."

"See, that's where I'm stuck."

"Stuck?"

"Is it really bad to work all the time if you love what you do?"

"Are you talking about my dad?"

She shakes her head.

"Yourself?"

She nods, her mouth set in a grim line. "Also, we don't really have much in common besides sex."

"True, but we work together all day—"

"Not. Any. More." She's back to poking me, one for each syllable.

Undeterred, I continue with my point. "Which means it's good to have other pursuits with other people outside of work to balance that out."

"Do we?"

"Work together? Or balance each other out?"

"Both. Either." She slaps her palms onto her face. "Ugh! I am so confused."

I'll be honest, I'm relieved she's no longer poking me, but I hate to see her hurt herself, so I gingerly take her hands in mine. "Do you want to maybe go out to the car to continue this? Go get some breakfast?" She looks so lost I just want to hold her. "Or do you want to just sit down here?"

She gestures to the living room. "There's only one chair."

I take a quick look around Ford's apartment, even more scantily furnished than mine. "You take it. I'll sit on the floor."

Once she sits, all the oomph seems to leak out of her, and my heart just gives it all up. I adore fierce Violet, but overtired and overwhelmed Violet brings out some other kind of love in me. The kind that just wants to take care of her. "So where were we?"

"I don't know." She shakes her head slowly. "Something about a fatted calf?"

"Oh, I remember. I was explaining what changed my plans."

She nods slowly. "Riiight."

"I fell in love with someone."

Her brows come together. "You did? Who? Do I know her?"

It's hard to tell if she's kidding or not until one side of her mouth quirks the tiniest little bit. I pull her out of the chair and onto my lap. "You little minx. What am I going to do with you?"

"I can think of a few things, but I think I need to hear it for real first."

"You mean like this?" I shift to face her and take her hand. "Violet Whatever-Your-Middle-Name-Is—"

"Rose."

"Two flowers? Really?"

"They couldn't decide."

"Interesting. Anyway, Violet Rose Davenport, I am in love with you. And to that end, I'm wondering if you might hire me."

"For sexual favors?"

He rolls his eyes. "I'm pretty sure you'll still get those for free. But you, my dear, are the one with the casting company now, and as of today you've got far more work than you and Betty can handle. Also, I could use a job."

"But you hate casting."

"I'm not a fan of some aspects of it, especially the part that throws me back into the throes of my unrequited adolescent need for my dad's attention, but I like other parts. Also, I don't have to be passionate about my job. I've got other passions."

"Like me?"

I nod, fighting a smile. "Like you. And surfing. And the environment. I have some plans to address the latter two."

"What about me?"

"Well, that depends."

"On what?"

"On whether you give me a job or not."

She squeezes her eyes shut. "You said something. On the phone. You left a message Saturday morning. About your dad."

I think back to that phone call. "I told you everything in the message."

She wrinkles her nose. "The machine ate it."

"Ate the message?"

She nods, then shakes her head. "Yes. No. It ate the tape. I didn't hear it all."

"Well, it was basically that he actually listened to me. That's why he agreed to close up shop. We talked a lot Saturday morning, and I think we worked through a lot of old misunderstandings."

"But you still want to leave California?"

"Yes. But for once, I'm not running away from it. From him or from failure. Or pain. I'm running *to* something. At least, I will if I can find a job in Wallington."

She purses her lips and taps a finger on them for a long moment. "I guess I could hire you. On one condition."

"What's that?"

"You sign some sort of 'it's okay to be sexually harassed by my boss' clause because…"

"You won't be able to keep your hands off me?"

She shakes her head. "Not for ten hours in a row."

I shake mine. "I work eight, max."

"We'll negotiate your workday. But it doesn't matter. Turns out I can't go any hours without having my hands on you." She taps her skull. "It obviously makes me nutso."

Trailing a finger down my cheek and along my jaw she adds, "You know why?"

I shake my head again.

"Because I'm in love with you too."

"At least we can agree on the love thing." I wipe my hand across my brow. "Phew."

She pokes me again before planting a long, luscious kiss on me. Sometime later, she breaks the kiss to ask, "So what do we do now? I've got a whole day left in the City of Angels."

"You mean after I give you this?" I ask, pulling a velvet bag from my pocket.

Her brows come together when I hand it to her.

"Open it."

She pulls the drawstrings open and dumps the contents onto her palm. Lifting the gold chain with the heart-shaped sea glass suspended from a nest of spun gold, she examines the necklace. "Where did you get this?"

"I found it at Wrightsford. The sea glass, anyway. It made me think of you, so I asked a surfer I know who makes jewelry to turn it into a necklace."

"It's beautiful," she whispers as she undoes the clasp.

"Here, let me do it."

She leans forward and lifts her hair so I can hook the clasp behind her neck. After sitting back against the wall, one hand presses the sea glass against her sternum, the other takes my hand, and she turns to face me.

"When you wear it, you'll know that I'm thinking about you."

"What if I wear it all the time?"

"I'd say that'd be just about right."

CHAPTER 19

Lawson's Reach, Season 2.

A death in the family, an accident, and a troubled marriage serve as the background to Lawson and Charli's new relationship.

VIOLET

Dani picks me up at the Wallington airport Monday evening, and the moment my butt hits the passenger seat of her car, she blurts, "Whitney's getting married."

I'm so startled I get tangled in the seatbelt. "What the hell?"

Dani looks over her shoulder and pulls away from the curb while Skye sticks her head between the front seats to greet me enthusiastically. Her soft fur is a comfort, but my heart's still racing. "Are you going to explain?"

Dani shakes her head. "I need to get to the beach. Can we go there before I take you home?"

"All right, but you better fill me in on the way."

She navigates to Wrightsford Avenue, and before I know it, marshes are flying by on either side of us as Dani tells me what she heard.

"I went by my mom's house to borrow her weed whacker. She was at the hairdresser yesterday, and Whit's mom came in all atwitter. Couldn't help overhearing her 'cause you know how she is when she wants everyone to know her business."

"Loud and over-the-top?"

She nods, but then shakes her head. "Apparently, she was there to book the salon to do Whitney and her bridal party's hair and makeup for her wedding on August 29."

"August *1998*?"

"She didn't say, but my mom said they were having to reschedule other appointments, so it sounds like this month and not a year from now, yeah."

"Who the hell is in her bridal party?"

"Not us, obviously. But isn't the bigger question, Who the hell is she getting married to?"

As I wait for her to answer, my gaze is caught by a heron flying over Bradley Creek. Outside of the manicured lawns of Beverly Hills, the landscape in Los Angeles was dry and desert-like, which I hadn't expected. The greens and blues on either side of us now soothe my eyes, but my gut clenches more tightly with every passing mile. When we get to the bridge to Wrightsford Beach and she still hasn't answered her own question, I clear my throat. "Do you know? Who she's marrying?"

She shakes her head no but says, "Unfortunately, yes."

"Is it Sully or Ford?" I can't see how either of them would've asked her without telling Dani or me, but one can always hope.

Still shaking her head, she finally answers. "It's that damn Hardy McRae."

"What? What the hell? I mean, I know his family owns half the town, but he's a total creep."

"Who comes from a long line of creeps," Dani says grimly.

My grandma said once that Whitney's family are the kind

of people that go to church every Sunday to be seen rather than to listen. That they're busy making sure they're the Joneses that nobody else can keep up with. But the McRaes take that to a whole other level. They've got parks and buildings and roads named after them, but I doubt there's an honest bone in any of their bodies.

"Whit complained a few times that her parents wanted to marry her off to a potential business partner," I say, still trying to absorb the news. "But I just thought she was being dramatic."

"I'm just going to park at the pier instead of driving to the north end," Dani says abruptly, pulling into the closest lot. The one we usually avoid because it's clogged with tourists. It's a Monday evening, though, so she manages to find a spot.

Moments later, we're out of the car and following the dog toward the water. Once our feet hit the sand, I ask, "What are we going to do?"

"I don't know if there's anything we can do."

When we get close to the hard-packed sand, Dani stops and just stares out over the waves, hands clasped on top of her head. "I feel awful. I'm worried that yelling at her like I did somehow led to this."

Skye must sense her distress because instead of pulling us towards the water, she presses against Dani, who squats to hug the dog. Despite the fact that I hate getting my clothes sandy, I plop down next to them and put my arm around my friend.

"Don't take that on yourself. Whitney's a grown woman who can make decisions for herself."

Dani winces. "Is she, though?"

I have no answer for that. We're all the same age, but Whit has always acted younger.

We don't really know how her parents raised her, besides the fact that they're always giving her expensive presents. From the time we were little, Mr. and Mrs. Moore always made it clear without actually saying so that we weren't welcome at their house. Pretty sure they think we aren't good enough for their princess. But Whit always found a way to hang out with us anyway.

Until now. Since that fight after the hurricane, she hasn't returned my calls. And honestly, I kind of gave up. Now I feel guilty about that. If I'd kept trying, could I have talked her out of this?

Dani shifts away from me suddenly. "Where's Nate?"

"He's still in LA."

"Like, for good?"

It's hard to tell if my friend hopes he's coming back or not. Things have moved quickly, and I wasn't even sure what was happening when I headed west myself. But I can't stop the smile that takes over my face. "He's just taking a couple days to pack up his stuff, and then he's moving here."

"Like, for good?" she asks again, but her tone has softened.

"We're going to take it all one day at a time, but I think so. He really wants to start a chapter of this thing he was involved with in California called the Surfrider Foundation. They do beach cleanups and lobby for wildlife protection, stuff like that."

"That's cool. What's he going to do for work?"

My smile grows even wider. "He's going to work for me."

She laughs. "That'll be interesting."

"I think it will, actually. We're a pretty good team."

She looks out over the water and frowns. "So does that mean you're not going to live with me?"

I squeeze her shoulder. "Actually, I was going to ask if I could move in this week. I think it's better to do it sooner rather than later."

"Are you sure you don't want to live with him?"

I shake my head. "I mean, I'm sure I'll be spending a lot of nights there, but it seems wiser for us to have our own space."

She cocks her head and raises a brow.

"I think we have a good chance of making it work, but I don't need to rush into it. I want to take time to lay the groundwork so we last. Plus, I was looking forward to living with you again."

She nods, and her gaze tracks back to the horizon. We sit in silence and just take in the roll of the waves for a bit. As it always does, this view slows my heart rate and soothes my soul. "I'm glad I still have you, Dan."

"Back atcha, Vi."

Skye barks, and I give her a hug. "You too, sweet girl."

It's full dark by the time Dani drops me off at my place. Before she can back out of the driveway, the light over the inn's side door opens and my grandmother calls, "Violet?"

I drop my bag at the base of the stairs. "I'm back. I was just going to drop off my stuff before I came over to check in."

She peers at the car in the dim light. "Is that Dani?"

"Yes, ma'am," Dani answers through the open window.

Gran clasps her hands over her round belly. "I need to talk to y'all."

Dani turns off her car and climbs out. "What's the matter?"

Gran looks between us before answering. "There's been an accident."

That's a wrap for Vi & Nate's love story, y'all, but the next book in the Carolina Classics series continues the journey for this group of friends:

Hold On To Me

https://books2read.com/HOTMKGrey

If you can't wait, you can also get a *bit* more info now with a bonus epilogue. You can get it at the link below after you sign up to be a Karen Grey VIP. (If you're already a subscriber, don't worry, you won't be subscribed again.)

https://books.bookfunnel.com/karengreyfreeforsubscribers

If you want more from Violet and her friends, turn the page to check out a sample from the novella, I'LL STAND BY YOU.

VIOLET

Wrightsford Beach, NC
August 31, 1991
9:35 p.m.

As I pour myself yet another cup of coffee, I try to remember why I'd thought it was such a good idea to add another job to my already jam-packed summer schedule. Today I woke at 9 a.m. in order to work an eight-hour day at my theater camp job, then had just enough time to change out of the T-shirt and shorts I wear as a counselor and into my Rumrunner Hotel attire—golf shirt and khaki skirt—and drive across town to begin my graveyard shift here at the front desk.

I'd hoped to recreate the summers of our early teen years, for my four best friends and I to spend quality time together before we all focused on finding real jobs in the real world. Like, wouldn't it be *so totally awesome* to work together at this hotel after college graduation just like we did after junior high graduation?

Back when we were fourteen, we thought we'd hit the jackpot when we all scored summer jobs at Wrightsford Beach's most popular resort. Just like on our favorite TV show, *Beverly Hills, 90210,* all we had to worry about was how deep we wanted our tans to be and whether to spend our wages on burgers or ice cream.

Unfortunately, just like *Melrose Place* vis-a-vis *90210,* the spin-off hasn't exactly lived up to the original. For all kinds of reasons.

No time to dwell on that, however, because duty calls in the form of a very handsome, very worried-looking man.

A number of guests are in tuxes because there's a wedding reception in the ballroom, but I'm 99 percent sure this partic- ular man in a penguin suit is the groom. Pasting on a profes- sional smile, I ask, "Is there something I can do for you, Mr. Smith?"

He seems surprised that I know his name, so I hold up the file. "I've got your event details right here, and I recognize you from the bridal party photo shoot. I never forget a face."

"Oh, well, thanks. I mean, yes, I hope you can help. My dog's gone missing."

"Dog?" Pets are allowed at the hotel, but I don't remember seeing anything about one in residence at the moment.

"We decided at the last minute to bring Ribsy to be our ring bearer." He drags a hand down his face. "I thought it would make my daughter happy, but if he's lost, we'll all be heartbroken."

Batting curiosity aside—not too many grooms his age have kids old enough to participate in their weddings—I pull out a pad of paper. "I totally understand. You wouldn't happen to have a photo of him, would you?"

He shakes his head. "Back home in Boston I have plenty, but nothing with me."

"Okay. Why don't you give me a description and the last place and time you saw him. I'll radio the staff to keep an eye out."

"He's a pretty typical-looking hound dog, mostly black with a brown face and legs and a few white spots. He's very friendly. Unfortunately, he'll follow anybody." He runs a hand through his hair, mussing it. "Uh, what else?"

"He was in the wedding with you?"

"Right. On the beach."

"And then what?"

"I took him up to the room and gave him his dinner. I just went up to take him out one last time to do his business, and he wasn't there."

A woman in a fifties-style blue dress exits the restrooms. When she notices Mr. Smith, she shifts course away from the ballroom doors and toward us. "Is everything okay, Henry?"

"Hey, Lucy. I hope so. Ribsy's missing."

"Oh no."

"Any ideas?" Turning to me, he explains, "Lucy trains dogs. Lucy, Ms."—he peers at my name tag—"Davenport has very generously agreed to spread the word."

I grab a marker and sketch out a "Missing Dog" flyer while they talk. They're halfway to the ballroom by the time I finish, so I quickly lock up my drawer and trot to catch up with them. "Excuse me, Mr. Smith?"

When he turns, his brow is still creased with worry. "Please, call me Henry."

We're not supposed to call guests by their first names, so I just hold up the paper in my hands. "It's a bit late to knock on doors, but if you like, I can make copies of this and we can put them up."

He looks like he's going to protest, but his friend intervenes. "That's actually a great idea," she says.

"Okay, then. Thank you. But I'm sure it's not part of your job description." He holds out a hand. "I'll make the copies in your business center and put them up."

"It's your wedding night, sir. I'm happy to take care of it."

I'm rewarded with a half-smile. "How about this? I'll go check in with my wife and see what she wants to do."

"That sounds like a wise plan." I hold up my walkie-talkie. "Meanwhile, I'll make copies and get the word out to staff."

"Thank you. We appreciate it."

"You're most welcome."

After pressing the talk button on my radio, I broadcast, "Ten-seventeen, I repeat, ten-seventeen." Knowing at least one staff member won't remember what this means, I add, "This is urgent. A guest's dog is missing. Please ten-forty-five on channel four. Ten-twenty-seven to four now. Over."

Switching to channel four, I hope that everyone will report in as ordered.

"Ford for Violet. Over."

"Go ahead, Ford. Over."

"I'm ten-twelve, but negative on the dog. Over."

Keeping it brief since ten-twelve means he's dealing with a guest out at the valet stand, I confirm that I've received the message. "Ten-four. Thanks, Ford. Over."

"I'll keep an eye out. Over."

Ford's one of my buddies-since-kindergarten who's working the hotel this summer. He's got that all-American hero thing going, so he'd never sit by while an unaccompanied dog ran away. But then I remember that he's working the valet stand on his own. The kitchen was short-staffed, so Sully, the other valet on for the night, offered to jump in there to help—meaning that a dog could've slipped out while Ford was parking a car.

Before I can ask him if he's still on his own, static lets me know I've got another report coming in.

"Dani for Violet. Over."

"Go ahead, Dani."

"I'm also ten-twelve. Lots of people at the bar. No dogs anywhere in sight all evening. Over."

"Ten-four, Dani."

Dani—short for Danielle—really lucked out with her job assignment this summer. At just twenty-two, she's mastered tending bar, from the drink making to the empathetic listening. She's always got her ears and eyes open, so if the dog does make it to the event ballroom, I can count on her to take care of the situation.

No one in the kitchen wears a radio, but I won't call over there until the dinner service is over. Chef wouldn't appreciate the interruption, and besides, any dog that set foot in his kitchen would be lucky to make it out alive.

No one else reports in with a dog sighting, so I fire up the copy machine. Something tickles my memory as I place the flyer on the glass, so once it's started spitting out copies, I take the first few and go back to the desk. After a quick scan of the event timeline, I have an idea of what might have happened.

Knowing that my sweet but scatterbrained friend Whitney has never mastered the walkie-talkie codes, I switch back to the main channel and try English.

"Violet for Whitney, come in, Whitney. Over."

Nothing but static.

"Please report to the front desk, Whitney. Over."

Static, then what sounds like giggling. "Whitney, what's your twenty? Over."

"Oh my god, Vi," Whitney finally answers. "Enough with the trucker talk."

"It's standard procedure, Whit. Over."

"It's idiotic is what it is. What do you—Hey, stop that! I told you to—"

The rest of her sentence is cut off by a squeal and then dead air. "Whitney, I'm not messing around. We have an emergency. Please report to the front desk. Now."

She may be one of my best friends, but the girl is a terrible maid and a worse flirt. I just hope she didn't let the dog out. Her family's connections got us in the door back in 1985 when all every teen in town wanted was to work at the beach. But even your daddy's influence can't save your job when you ignore every single rule.

When she doesn't answer, I lock up the desk and go looking for her.

Ready for more of this short and sweet introduction to the Carolina Classics friend group? Get it FREE by joining my VIPs at followkarengrey.com.

ALSO BY KAREN GREY

Hold On To Me

In this slow-burn, boss-assistant, entertainment biz romance, a bad cop movie production chief takes on a sexy assistant who challenges her every assumption. books2read.com/HOTMKGrey

What I'm Looking For

The course of true love never did run smooth, but in this smart and sexy retro rom-com with a finance-nerd heroine and a drama-geek hero, returns on love can't be measured on the S&P 500. books2read.com/WILFKGrey

Forget About Me

An underwear model, a best friend's little sister, and a dog who steals the show make for an unforgettable mix in this bittersweet romantic comedy. books2read.com/FAMKGrey

Like It's 1999, *a holiday novella*

Love 'em and Leave 'em Alice Kim and "Hot" Steve Lowell are perfect for each other. It'll only take them ten years to figure that out. books2read.com/1999KGrey

You Spin Me

If two lonely people fall in love over late-night phone calls, will meeting face-to-face make them, or break them? In this heartfelt, slow-burn retro romcom, it may be the end of a decade, but it's the beginning of a love story. books2read.com/YSMKGrey

Child of Mine

A single mom gets a job offer she can't refuse but has to work side-by-side with the one-night stand that doesn't know he's a father. Of her daughter. books2read.com/COMKGrey

ACKNOWLEDGMENTS

This book was brought to you by peanut M&Ms (both milk and dark chocolate). They were the 4pm snack that had me powering through the challenge of starting a new series and writing an enemies-to-lovers book (harder than you'd think, y'all. At least for me.)

What really kept me going? Knowing you were out there, reader! Especially those of you that have been on this journey with me more than once.

Editors Sarah Pesce of Lopt 'n Cropt and Jax Warren did their bits, cheering me on, and keeping the story and grammar in line.

As for research, my dear friends Regan Forman Gross and Amy Dawn spent hours on the phone with me, regaling me with stories of doing background and local casting in Wilmington, NC in the 1990s. Craig Fincannon patiently answered questions about running a casting office in the South in the late 20th century, and shared a great deal about the history of the film and TV biz in Wilmington. Jay Scully shared details about casting in LA. While I did draw on their stories for inspiration, I changed ALL the details to protect the innocent. (Although someone *did* rip up paperwork and dismiss background actors when they were being mistreated, with the words, "Get your own damn extras!") Of course, all errors are my own.

ABOUT THE AUTHOR

KAREN GREY is a *USA Today* bestselling and award-winning author of vintage romantic comedies with smart heroines and hunky heroes. Drawing on a long career as a performer, her retro 80's and 90's romances are populated with characters working both on- and off-stage in theater, TV and film. When not reading or writing, she's lounging at the beach or hiking in the mountains. Or dreaming about both with an IPA in hand and a dog or a cat nearby.

To get the latest news, join her VIP club at followkaren-grey.com.

(Author photo: Kate Mejaski)

For news, bonus material & a free book go to:
followkarengrey.com

facebook.com/karengreywriter
instagram.com/karengreywrites
goodreads.com/karen_grey
bookbub.com/profile/karen-grey

Made in the USA
Columbia, SC
18 January 2023

75508136R00135